CHADRON (NE) STATE COLLEGE
3 5086 00368383 4

THE BUDDY TRAP

Books by Sheri Cooper Sinykin

Shrimpboat and Gym Bags
The Buddy Trap

SHERI COOPER SINYKIN

ATHENEUM • 1991 • NEW YORK
Collier Macmillan Canada
TORONTO
Maxwell Macmillan International Publishing Group
NEW YORK OXFORD SINGAPORE SYDNEY

Library of Congress Cataloging-in-Publication Data

Sinykin, Sheri Cooper. The Buddy Trap / Sheri Cooper Sinykin.—1st ed. p. cm. Summary: Forced to spend the summer at a camp dominated by war games, Korean American seventh grader Cam endures the antagonism of tentmates and tries to keep secret his love for playing the flute. ISBN 0-689-31674-7 [1. Camps—Fiction. 2. Musicians—Fiction. 3. Korean Americans—Fiction.] I. Title. PZ7.S6194Ch 1991 [Fic]—dc20 90-49994

 Atheneum. Macmillan Publishing Company, 866 Third Avenue, New York, NY 10022. Collier Macmillan Canada, Inc., 1200 Eglinton Avenue East, Suite 200, Don Mills, Ontario M3C 3N1. First edition. Printed in the United States of America.

Printed in Hong Kong by South China Printing Company (1988) Ltd.

Printed in

1 2 3 4 5 6 7 8 9 10

To Rudi, my Sun

Acknowledgments

My thanks to Tom Deits, Doug Bradley, Lt. Fred Erickson, Mike Rule, and Gary Paulsen, for early readings of my manuscript; to Alison Bush for the music in Cam's soul; to Rene Hallen for moral support; and especially to my friend and mentor, Marion Dane Bauer, who helped me run with my dream.

THE BUDDY TRAP

ONE

MAYBE IT'S NOT too late. Maybe I can make them change their minds. Cam dropped his bags and raced toward the camp's parking lot. From the overlook, he spied his parents' Volvo. It hadn't budged. Not that Dad wasn't trying. He was hemmed in by an old VW van that kept wheezing and dying. Cam waved and slid down the pine needle–covered embankment.

"Hey, Dad! Mom! Wait up!" he yelled as he wove between the parked cars.

The VW coughed, then lurched forward. Seizing the opening, Dad gunned the engine. His tires spit gravel and churned up a cloud as he accelerated toward the exit and onto the unpaved road.

Cam charged after them. "Hey! Wait for me!"

Another car growled at him from behind. "You! Kid!

Get outta the road!" the driver yelled out the window.

Cam lunged for the shoulder, collapsing in a patch of blue wildflowers. The car swept past, and a gray glimpse of Volvo was swallowed up by the forest.

"Darn!" He ricocheted a rock off a nearby pine, sending bark chips flying. Drawing himself up, he confronted the Camp Rainbow Lake sign down the road. It might as well have said Camp Rambo Lake, from the looks of its brochure. Archery, shooting ranges, war games—those were the last things Cam wanted to do this summer.

How could Dad say, "Don't worry. You're gonna have a great time"? He must have known Cam would hate it here. Why else would he have been so apologetic when he hugged Cam good-bye?

"Will you just give it a chance, Cam? Please? For me?"

"But I won't fit in here, Dad. I'm different. Why can't I go to Interlochen? I'd get my concerto in half the time if I went there."

"You know what Mrs. Ellison said, son. You've hit a plateau. You're pushing yourself way too hard. She was very firm in recommending that you take the summer off and do something completely unrelated to music."

"But, Dad—"

"I know, Cam. I've got doubts about this, too. What if we're *not* doing the right thing in sending you?"

"You're not. Believe me."

"I don't know. Somehow I keep coming back to the same issue—trusting Mrs. Ellison where flute is concerned. You don't want to burn yourself out, do you?"

"I won't. I promise."

"Come on, Cam. Don't disappoint me now. I'm counting on you to have fun and make some new friends. You know what they always say: 'A man without friends is poor indeed.' "

Dumb slogans again. Just what Cam needed. Too bad he couldn't have countered with something equally catchy and wise; his own arguments had been futile. As far as his parents were concerned, Mrs. Ellison knew better than they did what was best for Cam. So what if he *was* getting frustrated, crying sometimes when the fingering wouldn't come? So what if he *had* thrown a few tantrums and skipped dinner a couple of times? Big deal. He wouldn't starve. How else would he ever improve if he didn't try harder and practice more? Mrs. Ellison had to be dreaming if she really believed taking the whole summer off would result in a breakthrough.

Now the midday sun pressed down upon him like a sizzling iron. At least it was a dry heat, and his skin and clothes could breathe. Not like most summers, when Wisconsin's humidity plastered his T-shirt to his chest for days at a time. Back home everyone was complaining, but what was so bad about forty-something days without rain? They acted as if banning the Fourth of July fireworks were the end of the world.

Cam felt in his pocket for the folded Interlochen brochure, reassuring himself that it was still there. His fingers caressed the slick paper as he glared up at the

Camp Rainbow Lake sign. Seven weeks. An eternity. With a great sigh, he pulled out the brochure and studied its picture collage for what to him seemed like the eighty-eleventh time. The kids who smiled back from behind their instruments looked like a United Nations delegation. How easy it'd be to blend right in. . . .

"Hey, you!" Cam turned to see Pee Wee, his counselor, loping toward him across the parking lot. The guy was anything but short, and had obviously chosen his camp name in jest. "Where in the world do you think *you're* going?" Pee Wee's hair was a tumble of sweaty-looking, blond curls. Concern etched his tanned face. Cam blinked up at him, unable to find words. "You *are* in Olympus, aren't you? Cameron Whitney, right?" Cam nodded, not bothering to offer his nickname. "If you wanted to take a nature walk, all you had to do was ask."

Cam refolded the brochure, avoiding Pee Wee's eyes. "I—I just wanted to ask my parents something."

"Guess you'll have to write them, huh? What've you got there?"

Cam stuffed the brochure into his pocket. "Nothing," he said. "Just some old flier."

As they charged up the incline from the parking lot, he surveyed the clusters of wood-framed tents that dotted the pinewood clearing. Boys were milling about, some in swimsuits, others in jeans. The *slap-smack* of a basketball in play shot toward them, while distant whistle-blowing trilled up from the lake, punctuating a rap tape on someone's boombox.

Pee Wee steered Cam back toward the junior high section of camp. "Did you get all settled?" he asked. "Got a bunk and all?" Cam shook his head. "Better hop to it then. We've got swim tests in fifteen minutes."

Pee Wee held open the screen door to a tent named Olympus as Cam gathered up his suitcase and sleeping bag. They were lying beside the nearby campfire ring, exactly where he'd dropped them in his haste to catch his parents.

Here goes nothing, he thought as he peered inside. Two sets of bunk beds lined each side. Pee Wee lifted the mosquito netting on one of the lower bunks and sat down, hunching forward to avoid hitting his head. Canvas tent flaps had been unrolled for privacy, and the scent of coconut suntan lotion just hung there, trapped in the stuffy dimness.

A tall blond guy lay sprawled on a top bunk. He clicked a new cassette into the boombox he'd wedged among the rafters. In an instant, heavy metal music screamed down at Cam. Of all the tents, he had to get this one. He bet the owner had never even heard of Mozart, much less owned a classical music tape.

Another kid was standing in the middle of the wood-planked floor, slathering lotion all over his already tanned body. His baggy, flowered trunks sagged below his ample belly, and, despite the heat, his dark hair stood stiffly at attention. Even slouching over to grease his thighs, the kid towered over Cam.

Oh well, Cam thought. His best friend, Denny Malzahn, had grown a foot taller since the beginning of sixth grade and it hadn't affected *their* friendship. The difference in height probably wouldn't bother these guys either.

Cam chose a lower bunk across from the others and unrolled his sleeping bag. As he patted out wrinkles, the mattress coughed up dust.

"Why don't you guys introduce yourselves?" Pee Wee yelled above the music. "I ought to go see what happened to the others." As he opened the door, another kid appeared as if on cue. "Well, speak of the devil."

"Hey, Pee Wee Man, thought you'd try another summer, huh?" Cam was relieved to see that the new arrival, dressed all in black, from his fedora to his high-top sneakers, was only slightly taller than he was. Beneath the felt brim, the kid's eyes were flecked with mischief.

"Which one are you? I forget," Pee Wee said, consulting his clipboard. "Jason or Buddy? I figured neither of you guys would be back."

"You mean Buddy Fiedler's coming, too?" Jason rolled his eyes. "And he's in *my* tent?"

Pee Wee nodded. " 'Fraid so."

"Give me a break, will you?" Jason groaned. He dragged a huge nylon gym bag across the floor toward Cam's bunk.

"Well," Pee Wee said, "you guys get acquainted and I'll go find Buddy."

"Don't do us any favors," Jason muttered as the door slapped shut. He extended his hand to Cam, palm up.

"Jason Lowman," he said. "As in Willie. *Death of a Salesman*—except with a *w.*"

Cam plastered on a smile, nodding as if he knew the book or movie or whatever it was, and slapped him five. "Oh, yeah. Right. I'm Cam Whitney."

"Hey, Blondie!" Jason hollered across the tent. "Turn it down, will you?"

The kid on the top bunk grinned and lowered the volume. "Name's Mick. Alexander."

"As in the Great?" Jason said.

"Right."

"Jonah Wainwright," the dark-haired kid said. "As in nobody famous." He looked down at his stomach and smiled ruefully. "But you may as well call me Whaler. Everyone else does."

"Far out! A guy with a sense of humor. I like that." Jason elbowed Cam in the ribs, and Cam nodded his approval. Not that Cam found the nickname—or Jonah's resignation to it—funny. Poor guy. He probably figured Whaler beat Blubber, that he'd better make his preference clear from the start. Still, Cam couldn't imagine himself asking to be called No Nose or Flat Face, both names he'd overheard himself called at school.

Not to mention those other names—*gook* and *dink.* Those were the ones that *really* made his cheeks burn with shame, as if somehow he were less than the other kids just because of the way he looked. Cam thought fleetingly of Tyson Hardy, this black kid in his class who'd decked an eighth-grader for calling him "nigger." And of Tom Phan, whose family had escaped from Vietnam after the fall of Saigon. Anyone laying the name "gook" on Tom would be eating knuckles come recess time.

Cam chided himself at the memories. Why couldn't he be more like Tys and Tom? Why couldn't he do something besides slink away, pretending not to have heard those hurtful names? Was it because he didn't know enough about his real heritage to feel pride in defending it—or because his father was always telling him, "Go along to get along"? When it came right down to it, maybe he just couldn't ignore the Whitney Family Motto. . . .

Cam pushed aside the nagging thoughts and forced a smile for the guys' benefit. He'd make Dad proud of his efforts to win new friends if it was the last thing he did. Cam figured he owed his father at least that much—and probably a whole lot more. After all, Dad and Mom *had* saved him from who-knew-what-kind-of-life in that faraway orphanage.

Jason pointed to the bunk above Cam's. "Anyone got dibs on the top?" Cam shook his head. "Good. I get claustrophobia. Acrophobia, too. But—hey!—this isn't *that* high, right?"

"Right," Cam said. A snappy comeback, that's what he needed. Something to show Jason that he was no dummy either. What was the word that meant fear of open spaces? It started with *a*. His great-aunt Margaret had it. Cam ransacked his memory, could hear his mother saying the word, syllable by syllable, telling him to repeat it back to her. Yeah, that was it. "Good thing you're not agoraphobic," he added at last.

Jason pushed back his hat. His pudgy cheeks looked like someone had just pinched them. "Far out! Another candidate for Mensa!"

"Yeah, that's me all right," Cam said, even though he had only a vague idea what Mensa was. Something for smart people. A club, his mother had once said.

Jason unzipped his bag, pulled out a bedroll, and slopped it onto the mattress. A silvery square of cardboard dropped at Cam's feet. Bending over to pick it up, he discovered a matchbook engraved with the word *Einstein's*. He handed it to Jason, who palmed it gratefully. "For my collection," he said. "I've got nine hundred eighty-six others at home. But this seemed kind of fitting, you know?"

Cam nodded, pretending that Jason's genius was obviously equal to Einstein's. What harm could there be in flattering the guy?

"Great restaurant," Jason said. "We ate there on the way over." He cocked his head, appraising Cam's crimson Stanford T-shirt, a gift from his cousin. "So, do you go to a school for gifted kids too?"

"Me? No."

"Really?" Jason said. "I just figured—"

"Not that I couldn't." Cam's mind raced for an excuse. "It's just that my parents, well, they—"

"Parents." Jason sighed in commiseration. "Say no more. They're into public education, right?"

Cam nodded quickly. Why hadn't he thought of that? Mom and Dad were both professors at the University of Wisconsin, after all. They *had* to believe in public education. The public was paying their salaries. Besides, it was a better excuse than admitting that his good grades were the result of hard work—not a super-high IQ.

"What'd you say your name was?" Jason asked. "Kim?"

"Cam, short for Cameron."

"You must be adopted, right? What are you? Vietnamese?"

Cam shook his head. His cheeks flushed. He could feel the other boys' stares. Did they want him to be Vietnamese or not? He couldn't tell, and opted for the truth. "No," he said, "Korean."

"Oh. Korean." Jason nodded as if the single word explained everything. But even if Jason *did* know more about Korea than Cam did, that didn't mean he knew *anything* about Cam.

"Actually," Cam said, trying not to sound defensive, "I'm American."

"Well, of course." Jason chuckled nervously and glanced at Mick and Whaler. "I—we knew that."

Good, Cam thought. He hadn't turned the guys off by coming on too strong.

Whaler stepped away, pulled a crayon drawing from his suitcase, and taped it to the frame of the upper bunk. "You guys better hurry up and get dressed," he said. "Or am I the only one going swimming?"

Mick mumbled something but made no move to change out of his muscle shirt and wild beach shorts. Jason, on the other hand, began flipping clothes out of his gym bag all over the floor.

Cam unzipped his suitcase and pulled it clear of Jason's mess. Nestled on top between his beach towel and a sweatshirt was his black leather flute case. He covered it with a T-shirt, then glanced around quickly. Had anyone seen it? That was all he needed—being teased for seven weeks about bringing his flute. "What a nerd," they'd say. He could hear it all now. It wasn't easy being a classical music lover in a rock 'n' roll world, but Cam knew from past experience that it could be done. Hadn't he mastered the art of blending in at school? You bet: Except for a few close friends and the other kids in band, no one even knew that Cam played flute—let alone that he, a lowly sixth grader, had beaten out a hotshot eighth grader for first chair. With a little planning and imagination, Cam thought, the guys at camp would never have to know either. . . . He was just pulling up his swim trunks when Pee Wee poked his head in.

"Buddy's on his way down the hill," he said, "and, well . . ." The counselor cut himself off with a shake of his head. "Look, I'm sorry to bug out on you right now. But I really had better walk the Fiedlers back to their car. Be cool, Jason, okay?"

"Who me?" Jason rocked back on his heels with exaggerated innocence. "I'm always cool, Pee Wee Man, you know that."

"Uh-huh." Pee Wee winked at Cam as if they shared a secret. "You keep an eye on this guy, will you?"

"Count on me," Cam said, passing his own wink to Jason. Wouldn't want him to think Cam was playing up to the counselor. "What's with this guy Buddy?"

"You'll see," Jason said. "I guarantee it."

Cam's pulse quickened as the door squeaked open. Instinctively, he slipped onto his bed, into the shadows, as Buddy plunked his suitcase on the floor and drop-kicked his sleeping bag toward the empty bunk near Cam's and Jason's. Mick slid to the floor and extended his hand to Buddy.

"You're new, huh?" Buddy said. "Where you from?"

"L.A."

"All right!" Buddy slapped him five. He was almost as tall as Mick but gangly looking, as if his muscles hadn't quite caught up with his bones. His hair hung like straw, glossy and straight, over one eye. He flipped it back with little effect and nodded a greeting at Whaler. At last his gaze fell on Jason, whom he regarded coldly with his dark, uncovered snake-eye. "Not you again, geek," he said.

Cam drew in a sharp breath, let the word echo in his mind. No, it's okay. He said *geek* not . . . the Name. And he's talking to Jason. Let it go.

"Shut up, Fiedler," Jason said.

"I don't shut up, I grow up. And when I look at you, I throw up."

"How original!" Jason said. "Cameron, my good man, take down that quote, will you?"

Cam cringed, and inched out of hiding. Buddy stepped toward him, grating a rectangular ID tag against the neck chain from which it hung. Back and forth, back and forth. Tough. "Cam-moron," he said. "Now *that's* original."

Cam steeled his courage and returned Buddy's gaze. Exposed by his swim trunks, Cam's knees were Jell-O. He hoped Buddy wouldn't notice. Keep it light, play a role, play along. He forced a smile. "Most people call me Cam," he said.

Buddy tossed his hair, only to have it veil his eye once more. "You got that wrong," he said.

Cam swallowed hard, bracing himself for whatever Buddy was going to say. He took a step backward toward Jason. Mick and Whaler closed the circle on either side of Buddy. Their faces seemed to grow, change, and blur as Cam blinked up at them. "I—I don't know what you mean," he stammered.

"What I mean," Buddy said evenly, "is that most people call you 'gook'!"

TWO

CAM'S HEART HAMMERED in his ears as the faces swam into focus. Play it cool, play along, he reminded himself. But his stomach knotted at the suggestion. Now was the time to let Buddy have it, just the way Tom Phan would. But what about Dad? How could Cam purposefully disappoint him? He could just imagine the look on his father's face—and the great sigh Dad'd heave, filling him with shame. Maybe Cam should just pretend that he hadn't heard, turn the other cheek. Like always.

"He's Korean, Buddy," Jason said. "Don't you know anything?"

"Big wow. A gook by any other name—"

"Shut up, Fiedler!" Jason glared up at the taller boy.

Cam thought he should at least say something, make

some small attempt at defending himself. But words refused to come.

"What's the matter with you?" Buddy said, turning his eye back on Cam. "Don't you speak English?"

"Leave him alone, man," Whaler said.

"What's it to you, Blubber Belly?"

Whaler stepped in front of Cam, walling Buddy from view. "You wanna say that again?"

Mick nudged Buddy and nodded toward the door. "Pee Wee," he said. "Right outside."

Buddy scowled and backed off. Cam and Jason grabbed their towels and edged past him. Whaler straight-armed the door.

"Later for you guys," Buddy hissed.

"Promises, promises," Jason muttered.

As they headed toward the campfire ring where Pee Wee stood with another counselor, the sun stabbed Cam's eyes. His skin tingled from its warmth. He regarded Jason incredulously. "You actually *like* getting into it with him, don't you?" The guy had to be crazy.

Jason shrugged. "You do what you've gotta do."

"Yeah, but . . ." Cam gathered up his admiration. "I can't believe the way you stand right up to him."

"What's he gonna do? Blow me away?" Jason laughed. "You guys stick with me and we'll make hamburger out of Buddy Fiedler."

Whaler's chuckle came out like a snort. Cam nodded his assent, but his stomach turned at the analogy. Buddy might be a jerk, but Cam had no desire to make him into anything but a nice guy.

"You all ready?" Pee Wee said. "Where are the others?"

"Shaving their legs." Jason grinned while Whaler snickered behind his fist. Cam forced his lips upward.

Pee Wee rolled his eyes. "Lowman, give me a break." Retreating into the tent, he returned moments later with Buddy and Mick.

Though Rainbow Lake was visible from the knoll outside Olympus, the waterfront itself lay just beyond the main lodge. Cam fell in step with Jason and tagged after the others. He mentioned that Mick still hadn't changed out of his shorts, and that he'd forgotten a towel.

"Hey, Surfer Boy!" Jason called. "Forget something?" When Mick didn't respond, he added, "Yo, Mick! Where's your surfboard?"

The blond boy flashed a Colgate smile over his shoulder but said nothing.

"Weird." Jason shrugged. When they reached the waterfront, he whipped off his black robe and modeled his matching trunks for Cam. If Whaler was the Sta-Puf Marshmallow Man, Cam thought, then Jason was the Pillsbury Doughboy, short and soft bellied. He smiled at his analogy. "You like my style, huh?" Jason said. "And you thought good guys only wear white."

"Right." Cam followed Jason onto the pier. It rose and fell with the wake of a passing speedboat. A hint of dead fish—obviously washed ashore somewhere nearby—rushed by on the breeze. The waterfront counselor handed Cam a buddy tag with his name on it, instructing him to hang it on the board.

Buddy and Whaler hustled along the pier with up-curled toes, howling about how hot the deck was, and dove in without urging. Mick hung back. Jason nudged him from behind. "Surf's up," he teased. "Whatcha waiting for?"

Mick turned sideways to let Jason pass. "You."

"No, no." Jason bowed with an exaggerated sweep of his arm. "I insist. After *you.*"

Mick blew out a long breath. He combed his fingers through his hair. "Look, you were here last year, right? Do we have to take this test?"

"Piece of cake, man," Jason said. "Don't sweat it."

"You think I am?" Mick's Adam's apple bobbed.

"Well?" Jason made his eyes bulge for effect, and turned to Cam. "These surfers," he said, feigning exasperation. "They think just cuz they practically *walk* on water, they shouldn't have to test out." He punched Mick's biceps playfully.

"Get out of here, will you?" Mick growled. "Where's the bathroom, anyway?"

Jason indicated the lower level of the lodge. "You can't miss it," he said. "Just follow your nose." Cam grinned, but Mick remained stone faced. "That was a joke, big guy. As in funny, ha-ha. Jeez! I can see I've got my work cut out for me."

Mick said nothing, but jogged off toward the lodge. His pinched expression and slouching posture made

Cam wonder whether he felt sick to his stomach. Maybe the heat had soured his lunch. . . .

"Shouldn't we turn his buddy tag?" Cam said. "If they take a head count, they might think he drowned or something."

"Yeah." Jason flipped Mick's tag and started toward the testing area. "Aren't you coming?"

Cam eyed the lodge and bit his lip. Mick sure was in a hurry to reach the bathroom. If he *was* sick, maybe he'd want Pee Wee to know. Or the camp nurse. Maybe he'd need some Pepto-Bismol. Cam could fetch a couple tablets from his suitcase. "Be there in a minute, Jason." Turning his own tag, Cam added, "Tell Pee Wee I'll be right back."

"Hey, what's up?" Jason called after him, but Cam, already charging up the path, didn't bother to reply.

The lodge's concrete slab floor was dark where it had been swabbed with disinfectant. The sharp smell and a dank chill hung in the air. Cam shivered as he hustled across the deserted expanse and into the lavatory.

There was no sign of Mick. Cam called his name, and it bounced back, unanswered, from the metal stall dividers. He wrinkled his forehead. The only other place Mick could be was in the shower. Fat chance. But turning the corner into the L-shaped alcove, Cam spied deck shoes protruding beneath the shower curtain, and curly blond hair above.

"Hey. What are you doing in there?"

"Taking a shower," Mick shot back. "What do you think?"

"Without water? And with your shoes on?" Cam laughed. "What's that? A custom in California or something?"

"Right."

Cam sighed, considered his next move. What was Mick's problem? Why in the world was he hiding in here? "I don't get it," he said. "What's the matter? Are lake waves too small to bother with? Or are you just homesick for salt water?"

"Aren't you gone yet?"

"Uh-uh."

Mick flung open the curtain with an angry clash of hooks scraping metal. "What's *with* you, anyway?" Long lashes shaded the blue of his eyes. A fine, white fuzz covered his upper lip and cheeks. "Why aren't *you* swimming?"

"I—I was worried about you," Cam said. "I thought maybe something was wrong. Like, are you sick or what?"

"I'm fine," Mick said. "So you can beat it, okay?"

"B-but what should I tell Pee Wee?"

"Don't tell him anything. Just mind your own business."

Cam scowled. If he didn't know better, he'd think Mick was hiding more than himself. Was he chicken? No way. Everyone knew surfers practically *lived* in the water. "Look," he said patiently, "what's the big deal? You think just because it's a lake and not the ocean, you can't swim? Water's water. This stuff just tastes better."

"Who says I can't swim?" Mick shoved him aside, his eyes flashing.

Bingo, Cam thought. That's it. He *can't* swim! Amazing!

"Just go on. Get out of here."

"Okay, okay. In a minute." Cam stood his ground, but softened his tone. "I—I just want to help." Mick sighed, turned away, and paced to the sinks. Cam tagged after him, his heart thumping in his chest. Maybe if he taught Mick to swim, they could be friends. "Look," he said, "it's no big deal. I could teach you in twenty minutes. Easy."

Mick spun about. "Read my lips. I don't want to learn. And you'd better keep your little trap shut, you hear?" Cam gulped and nodded mechanically. "If anyone finds out, it's gonna be your head on a platter."

"But I was just—"

"Butting in where you don't belong," Mick said.

"You want me to tell Pee Wee anything?"

"Nothing. I'll make my own excuses." Mick nailed Cam with an icy stare.

Backing out of the rest room, Cam bumped his shoulder on the doorjamb. So what if Mick didn't like him; at least Jason did. And Whaler. "I—I won't say a word. I promise." Reeling about, he hurried toward the waterfront.

When Mick finally weaseled out of swimming by complaining about his allergies, Cam held his tongue. And he said nothing during supper when the Californian played up to Buddy with surfing stories about Malibu and Redondo Beach. But the whole charade made him sick. This wouldn't happen at Interlochen. There, what you saw was what you got. One big happy family. And everyone into music. He patted his pocket, felt the reassuring wad of brochure. In the middle of dessert, he excused himself and escaped to the bathroom below the mess hall.

Relieved to be alone, he locked himself in a stall and pulled out the brochure. A picture of Mick and Buddy, all palsy-walsy, superimposed itself over the one of the string quartet. Mick and Buddy, a team. That could wreck anyone's dinner. Not to mention an entire summer.

The ceiling pulsed with sudden activity—benches scraping, hundreds of feet beating their way to the door. Cam sighed. Wasn't there anywhere he could find some peace and quiet? Glancing again at the brochure, he refocused on the faces of the black violinist, the Asian cellist. No one would call him names there, he thought. For once in his life, he'd be among more than a few nonwhites. And whatever the campers' differences, making beautiful music would bring them all together. It'd be perfect.

All at once, the rest room door smashed open against the towel dispenser. "Where's Cam? He's gotta be down here." Laughter, mingled with screaming, distorted the speaker's voice.

They were after him! Cam fumbled with the brochure, his fingers like wood. Maybe he should climb up on the seat and duck his head. His mind and heart were racing.

"Whaler!" Jason barked. "Get his legs! That's it!"

"I'm gonna kill you guys. I swear. Put me down!" Buddy yowled like a cartoon coyote.

Puffing, scuffling, and a couple of curses echoed off the walls. "God, where's Cam? I thought you said he'd be here," Jason panted.

Cam cracked the stall's door. Buddy hung like a hammock between his two tentmates, and though he thrashed to free himself, Jason's leverage on his arms made his efforts futile.

"Hurry up!" Whaler said. "Before Mick finds us!"

"You guys are gonna pay for this, I swear!"

Jason's face reddened with the effort. "Jeez, where's Cam when you need him?"

Cam's heartbeat echoed in his ears. They needed him. But for what? An awful knot tightened around his dinner. He swallowed hard and popped out of the stall. "You rang?"

"Thank goodness," Jason said. "Here, give us a hand. You can be the flusher. Get back in there."

Cam retreated into the stall once more, pressing himself against the wall. Whaler and Jason squeezed Buddy in after him. "You guys give me a swirly and I swear I'll get you!" Buddy said. His voice ping-ponged off the walls.

"I owe you one from last summer, remember?" Jason managed between clenched teeth. "Okay, Whaler, lift his legs. Steady now."

Cam blinked in disbelief as Jason lowered Buddy's

head partway into the toilet. Whaler puffed under the strain of the added weight, his arms blanching as he tightened his grip around Buddy's thighs. "W-what are you guys doing?"

"What do you mean, 'you guys'? You're part of this, too," Whaler said.

"Yeah, but—"

"What are you waiting for, Cam?" Whaler nodded. "Do it!"

"What?" Cam's voice came out like a girl's. "Do what?" Now Buddy's hair was trailing in the blue water. His face was red and becoming redder by the second. Whaler readjusted his stranglehold on Buddy.

"Flush it, stupid! Hurry up! I can't hold him much longer."

Cam hesitated, licked his lips. *This* was their idea of fun?

"Come on, Cam. Chop chop." Jason flashed him a teasing grin.

There was no way out. If he didn't play along with them now, they'd write him off as a friend for sure. And then where would he be? Do it! Just do it! Cam watched his hand reach out, watched it push down on the metal handle. A chill raced up his arm.

Water rushed in, grumbling and gurgling, inching upward toward Buddy's eyebrows. Then, with a relentless sucking noise, it swirled about his head and was gulped down, along with Buddy's hair.

"Gonna . . . kill you . . . swear to God," Buddy

sputtered, his face crimson. From where Cam stood it was impossible to tell whether Buddy was panicked—or enraged.

Jason and Whaler were drunk with laughter, tears glistening on their cheeks. Cam pressed himself into the corner, wishing he could disappear magically into the concrete block wall. "Get him up!" Jason managed at last. "Let's see it."

Whaler lowered Buddy's legs and immediately seized his arms from behind, jerking them upward. Buddy spat at Cam, kicked at his captor, but couldn't connect as Whaler dragged him backward toward the mirror. "Cam," Whaler urged, "come out here and get a look at this!"

Play a role, play along, Cam told himself. Inching out of the stall, he suppressed a gasp. Buddy's likeness glared back from the mirror, his hair twisting upward like a unicorn's horn. A nasty, purple scar sliced diagonally over the eye that was usually covered with hair.

Buddy's gaze darted the width of the mirror, from Jason to Whaler to Cam. His face turned to stone.

"Come on," Jason said. "Let's get out of here."

Whaler released Buddy's arms and shoved Jason out the door. But Cam's feet were glued to the floor, his eyes, to the mirror.

Buddy's hands shot upward, pulled at his hair, rearranged it over his forehead. His eyes shone. "What are you staring at, gook?" The upraised angle of his jaw seemed to dare Cam to reply.

But all Cam could do was point. Even the word *gook*

did not distract him. At last he found his voice. "How . . . how'd it happen?"

Buddy whirled about and pressed his face close to Cam's. "None of your business." Cam flinched from the spray of Buddy's words as much as from his garlic-spiked lasagna breath. "Get this and get it good. You guys want trouble? Well, me and Mick, we're gonna give it to you."

THREE

LATER THAT NIGHT, after taps had silenced Jason's and Buddy's verbal warfare, Cam burrowed into his sleeping bag and shivered from its nylon chill. The raised tent flaps admitted a cricket serenade and inky darkness. His flashlight was a comforting lump beneath his pillow. He yawned, fighting sleep. If only he could wait them out, maybe he could sneak off and practice his flute.

Above him, the bedsprings groaned as Jason rolled over. Before long, slow, even breathing came from Mick's and Whaler's bunks. Raising up on one elbow, Cam strained to see Buddy's silhouette on the pillow in the next bed. Good, he thought. Peace at last.

Inch by inch, he unzipped his sleeping bag, then crept out into the cooling night air. The floorboards creaked as he crouched and began groping through his suitcase. At last he found his music pouch. His fingers caressed the rough leather flute case alongside. Drawing them both to his chest, he slipped into his sneakers and a windbreaker.

Mick mumbled something from across the tent. Cam's pulse quickened. He hugged his instrument protectively. Despite the cloaking darkness, he felt like an easy target. Was Mick awake? Had he seen the flute?

"Mick?" he whispered, but he didn't draw closer.

There was no reply, just steady snoring from the top bunk. Relieved, Cam rummaged beneath his bed for his backpack, stuffing the music and the flute inside all in one motion. Then he grabbed his flashlight, held his breath, and tiptoed toward the door. It opened and closed soundlessly.

Pee Wee and some other counselors were drifting toward the campfire ring from their staff meeting at the lodge. "Some Fourth of July," one said. "No fireworks. No nothing."

"It won't be so bad," Pee Wee said. "That new war game ought to be fun."

Cam rolled his eyes. A war game. Terrific. He pressed himself into the shadows and backed toward the gravel service road that snaked past Olympus, the camp director's cabin, and along the lake to the lodge. That was the long way—the dark way—to the bathrooms, but he couldn't risk Pee Wee spotting him and spoiling his plans.

Squaring his shoulders and facing the road, he hefted

his backpack and headed toward the lake without benefit of his flashlight. Gravel crunched underfoot. As he passed beneath a canopy of pines, wings ruffled the darkness overhead. In the director's cabin, pulled shades cast off comforting squares of amber light.

Clicking on his flashlight at last, Cam hustled along the waterfront. A breeze rose off the lake, riffling his hair. He faced into it, clutched his windbreaker tighter at the throat, and cut up toward the lodge.

Finding the door to the dining room locked, he proceeded to the recreation hall on the lower level. Though the dank chill of its concrete block construction seeped through the room, he was grateful for a buffer between himself and the night air. He closed the door. A dim light glowed overhead. Thank goodness the lodge was a long way from main camp. With all the windows shut, surely no one would hear him and come poking around. Setting his backpack and flashlight on the Ping-Pong table, he pulled out his case and began assembling his flute.

He was just searching through his music when the scrape of a door latch froze him in midmotion. A flashlight beam shot through the opening, nailing Cam in its glare. "What are you doing out alone? You're supposed to have a buddy." The voice hesitated, but the circle of light continued to grow. "What've you got there?"

Cam hid the flute beneath his windbreaker, squinted into the blinding beam. Guilt gnawed at his insides as if he'd been caught in midcrime. "Just . . . nothing."

It was Pee Wee who turned up the lights and shuffled

toward him. The counselor's gaze fell upon the open case and sheaves of music. He leafed through them and whistled. "You call this nothing? Looks hard to me," he said. "All these black notes. That means it's fast, right?"

"Very," Cam said, relaxing his grip on the instrument and easing it into view. The admiration in Pee Wee's eyes was easy reading. "Then you're not mad?"

"Mad?"

"About no buddy, remember?"

"Oh, yeah." Pee Wee rubbed his chin. "Well, just this once."

"But—" Cam sighed, interrupting his protest. "You don't understand. I need to do this *every* night."

"Don't you think you'll have time during the day? We do have free periods, you know."

Cam fingered a quick scale, frowned, and refitted the head joint. "It's not that. It's"—his mind searched for half-truths, not wanting to complain about Buddy and Mick—"kind of private," he said, "something I don't want getting around."

"Private, huh?" Pee Wee's quizzical expression made Cam squirm, but Cam volunteered nothing. At last the counselor shrugged. "Well, okay. If that's the way you want it, I'll try to cover for you. On one condition."

"Yeah? What's that?"

"You let me hear your stuff."

Cam smiled modestly. "You got a deal." He placed the silver instrument between his chin and lower lip, then raced through his warm-ups with flying fingers. The sweet clear notes tickled his soul, touched a special place within him that no thing or person ever reached. He closed his eyes—closed out Pee Wee's presence and Camp Rainbow Lake and Buddy Fiedler—and bathed in the pure emotion that worked its way up from the pit of his stomach to his chest to his throat. His eyes were hot and moist as he broke into the Mozart piece, joyous and free.

It wasn't perfect. He could see exactly where it needed work—where his fingers failed him, where his breath gave out. But at least he wasn't coming unglued about it. That was progress. He'd show Mrs. Ellison how wrong she'd been to make him take the summer off. If he kept working a little every day, he was sure to have it by fall—in time to ace first chair in the Youth Symphony tryouts.

"That was incredible!" Pee Wee breathed. "You really ought to play for the guys. They'd be impressed. I know it."

Cam shook his head. Forget it. He threaded his cleaning cloth through the eye of the metal prod and drew it through the flute. If he didn't go out of his way to show off his talent at school, why would he want to here at camp? Too much depended on his making friends, on the guys liking him. If he thought being here for seven weeks was going to be rough, seven *friendless* weeks were sure to feel like a life sentence.

"Maybe for talent night," Pee Wee suggested. "Just think about it."

Cam tried to imagine himself playing for Buddy and

Mick. Even for Jason. "I don't think so," he said. "They'd laugh."

"I doubt it. But suit yourself. Your secret's safe with me."

"Good," Cam said. "And as far as you know, my backpack's full of shampoo and junk, right?"

Pee Wee grinned. "Absolutely. I'll see to it you get the Clean Camper Award for all your late-night showers." He squeezed the back of Cam's neck playfully. "Don't be too long now. Reveille's nice and early."

As the counselor had predicted, seven o'clock came too soon. Before feet had even hit the floor, the tent was abuzz with speculation about how camp would celebrate the Fourth of July. Cam peeled out of bed without mentioning what he'd overheard last night. A new war game. He scowled, wishing it were just a bad dream.

"The heck with Independence Day," Jason said, dropping to the floor with a thunk. "It's my birthday."

"No kidding?" Whaler rolled out of the sack. He finger-raked his hair until it stood at attention. "Hey, you've always got a big celebration."

Buddy grunted and buried his face beneath his pillow.

"Come on, up and at 'em," Pee Wee said, batting away his mosquito netting so he himself could get up. "Fun starts right after breakfast. Buddy, Mick, get a move on."

Cam wriggled into a fresh T-shirt and jeans before

Mick and Buddy were awake enough to start hassling him about anything. Jason scrounged up the all-black outfit he'd worn yesterday and laid it on his bed. As Jason pulled his pajama top over his head, Buddy rocketed out of bed and grabbed up Jason's clothes. Cam pawed the air in vain, trying to retrieve them for Jason, as Buddy snatched them out of reach, wadded them up, and heaved them across to Mick, who stuffed them in the rafters.

"Hey! What the . . ." Jason's face reddened as Whaler pointed out the black ball near Mick's boombox. "All right. Give 'em back."

Mick grinned. "We thought you'd want to wear your birthday suit."

"Oh sure."

"Come on," Pee Wee said. "Throw 'em down here. Now."

Mick tossed the clothes down and Jason hurriedly put them on. "We'll think of something real special for you, Jase," Buddy said. "Don't worry. We won't forget your birthday."

"Oh, please." Jason rolled his eyes. "Don't do me any favors."

"I promise," Buddy said, crossing his heart with mock solemnity. "We won't."

After breakfast, Cam and the others followed Pee Wee across the playing field, past the Swamp, and up the hill to the main campfire ring. Logs were stacked like a tepee within the circle of rocks, but Cam figured they were just for effect. With the drought, there was no way they'd be roasting marshmallows out here.

Cam settled in between Whaler and Jason, who sat cross-legged and expectant, waiting for Mountain Man to begin. The burly camp director looked as if he'd escaped off the screen of a Disney wilderness movie, and, judging from the motley tuft of beard that reminded Cam of a mountain goat's, he had to be way older than Pee Wee and the other counselors. Maybe even forty.

At last Mountain Man held his hand aloft and conversation quieted. "We've got a new war game this year," he announced. Returning campers cheered. Cam shook his head and suppressed a scowl. War games. Of all the stupid ways to waste time. Mountain Man waited for everyone to settle down before continuing. "It's called Spoils of War." The boys whispered and made comments about the name among themselves. "Anyone know what spoils of war means?"

Something damaged by war, Cam thought, but didn't raise his hand. Jason nudged him. "You know, don't you?" he said, waving his. "Mountain Man, hey! Over here!"

No one else volunteered. Mountain Man grinned through his scraggly beard. "Okay, Webster," he said, indicating Jason.

"Spoils of war are goods or property seized from the enemy after a military victory." Jason boomed out the answer. His self-satisfied grin seemed to deafen him to Buddy and the other guys' snickers.

"Very good!" Mountain Man winked at Jason. "So, the object of the game is for each team to find things in the woods—you know, old soda cans, tires, bottle caps—and to keep them from getting taken by other teams. Once your enemy catches and tags you, he is allowed to pick one of your spoils. Then he must release you. When we ring the activity bell up by the lodge, your spoils are safe until the next time we play."

"When's that?" someone shouted.

"You'll see." Mountain Man's eyes twinkled mysteriously. "Just to keep you on your toes, we'll play several sessions over the next couple of weeks."

"How many on a team?" one kid called out.

"I was thinking tent against tent but—" Hissing and booing interrupted him.

"Too easy to get caught," one of the older boys yelled.

"Yeah, we need more like patrols."

Mountain Man stroked his beard and looked to a few of the counselors as if for advice. "Well," he said at last, "I suppose we could have two or three to a team. Sure, that'd be okay."

"What *is* this?" one kid grumbled. "A cheap way to get camp cleaned up?"

"Sounds that way to me," said another.

Cam listened to the debate, amused that everyone was getting so stirred up about what to him seemed like a scavenger hunt aimed at helping the environment. He had no problem with that, but why did they have to call it a war game? Was that the only way they figured they could get the guys fired up about playing?

"I don't get it," Buddy blurted, without raising his hand. "Where are we supposed to find all this stuff?"

"Good point. As you know, we back up to the national forest, and, unfortunately, not all folks leave their campsites the way they found them. With today being the Fourth of July, I'll bet you won't have any trouble finding spoils."

"What about boundaries?" one of the counselors asked.

"Anywhere in camp, of course, and as far as the ranger's road. See, what we're really trying to do here is some public service. After we've played all the sessions, two counselors and I will judge which team has the most unique spoils. You got it?"

Heads bobbed and someone yelled, "What's the prize?"

Mountain Man rubbed his hands together. "So glad you asked. Here's the deal. The winning team will be declared 'camp generals' and can give orders for two days!"

Cam bit his lip and his eyes widened. Camp generals. Now *that* was tempting! How he'd love to make Buddy and Mick wash pots and pans for six meals straight! But that'd mean playing the stupid game, and he could not imagine himself doing that.

"Cam, can you believe it? A way to get them!" Jason said.

"I bet we could." Whaler's lumpish face came alive. "The three of us against Mick and Buddy? No problem."

"I don't know." Cam shook his head. What if Buddy and Mick won? He shuddered at the thought. He and the others'd be scrubbing worse things than pots and pans—toilets maybe. With their toothbrushes. While Buddy stood over them with a whip.

"Well?" Jason said. "What do you think? Are we a team?" His eyes connected with Whaler's. Cam squirmed in the middle. Choosing sides would only make things worse. What did they need him for anyway? Why couldn't he just be neutral, like Switzerland?

"Look," Jason said patiently as if he were talking to a two-year-old, "don't you want to do your part for the environment? What do you want those guys to think? That you're un-American?"

Cam wagged his head from side to side. I'm as American as the rest of you guys, he thought, surprised at his own defensiveness. Was Jason just kidding around? Or was he really trying to make Cam squirm? Cam wished he could tell, but the perpetual twinkle in Jason's eyes gave no clue.

"So? Are you with us?" Whaler said.

Cam sighed. "Why don't we just pick up stuff and throw it away? Why does it have to be a war?"

"It's not a war," Jason said. "It's a *game.* You're missing the whole point. Kick back, man. Have some fun. This is camp, remember?"

Where had he heard that before? Oh yeah. Dad. "We

just think you need to expand your horizons a little. Kick back. Try some new things. Make some new friends."

"But what if the guys—"

"Don't worry, Cam. They'll like you."

Cam studied Jason's and Whaler's expectant faces. They *did* like him, he realized. Maybe he should just play along and not make waves. Besides, he *would* be doing his bit to help the ecology. He could try to ignore the war stuff, forget it even existed. Who could tell? Maybe the whole competition thing would turn out to be fun. Just as Dad said.

"Earth to Cam. Earth to Cam," Jason said. "Come in, Cam."

Cam sighed. There was no way he wanted his dad saying that Cam hadn't given this his best shot. What could it hurt to give the dumb game a try? "All right," he said, reluctantly letting go of being Switzerland. "I guess you can count me in."

FOUR

"YOU'VE GOT TO wear camouflage, man," Jason said as they tramped down the hill from the main fire ring toward Olympus. "Don't be stupid. You wanna be a walking target?"

"Give me a break." Cam grimaced. Jason was taking this as seriously as if it *were* a war.

"All right, maybe not a target. But you get my point."

"So what if I do?" Cam said. "I didn't bring any. Heck, I don't even *own* any. Wouldn't be caught dead wearing dumb old army clothes." Calm down. What was the big deal?

"Man, lighten up." Jason slung his arm about Cam's shoulders. "I brought an extra set. You'll thank me later."

"Terrific," Cam said without enthusiasm. Jason's

shadow, wider and slightly taller than his, marched ahead, just after Whaler's. Wearing Jason's clothes was going to be a joke, Cam thought. In more ways than one.

When they reached the tent, Buddy had already changed into a flak jacket and mottled trousers. Mick wore faded blue jeans and an olive green sweatshirt.

"Don't be shy," Buddy was saying. "My old man gave me a couple pairs. You sure you don't want one?"

"I move better in jeans." Mick grinned. "Thanks anyway."

Cam, relieved to be ignored by Buddy, hustled over to await his change of clothes. The sharp odor of urine wafted up from Jason's sleeping bag. Cam wrinkled his nose, studied Jason for a hint of recognition, embarrassment. He noted neither, and looked to Whaler for confirmation.

Whaler nodded, but said nothing. He drew closer to the bunk, and pointed out a dark circle in the center of Jason's bedroll.

Cam frowned. Surely if the stain had been there before, they would have noticed. And in this dry heat, it would have evaporated by now. Besides, how could anyone soak through to the *top* of the bedding? No, there was something fishy going on here. He looked askance at Buddy and Mick.

"P.U." Buddy said, his snake-eye trained on Jason. "Sure stinks in here."

Jason emerged from his gym bag with the camouflage clothes and sniffed the air. "Don't tell me, Fiedler," he said. "You didn't pee your bed, did you?"

"No, but *you* did." Buddy hooted. "What's the matter, Lowman? Couldn't hold it till morning?" Jason's eyes narrowed into an expression of pure loathing. "Didn't I promise you a happy birthday?" Buddy chortled.

Jason checked his sleeping bag and cursed. "All right, Fiedler. What did you use?"

Buddy smirked at Mick, who eyed the floor. "What do *you* think?" Buddy said.

"You didn't! You wouldn't!"

"Make you a bet." Buddy smirked.

"God, you're disgusting!" Jason said. "Not to mention unoriginal. At least last summer I used ammonia on yours. Faked you out pretty good."

"Yeah? And yesterday you gave me a swirly. You had it coming."

Mick chewed off a fingernail and spat it on the floor. "Come on, Buddy. Let's go."

Buddy backed toward the door. "Yeah. We've got a war to win. See you around, suckers."

After they'd gone, Jason eyed his sleeping bag ruefully. "Thought you said this was a game," Cam said. "Here, let me help. Maybe we can wash it out up at the lodge."

Whaler pinched a fold of sleeping bag. "No way it'll dry by tonight."

"Don't be so sure," Jason said. "Alls I have to do is get Pee Wee to let us use the staff laundry. Simple."

"You mean you're going to tell on Buddy and Mick?" Cam said, his eyes wide. "You think you ought to?"

Jason shrugged. "I'll do what I've gotta."

Cam shook his head, imagining Pee Wee coming down on Buddy and Mick, imagining them coming down on him, Jason, and Whaler. But in the end, all Jason said was there'd been an accident, and Pee Wee, sympathetic, offered to wash and dry the sleeping bag himself. Now Cam struggled after Jason and Whaler as they pressed east toward the national campground.

"Let's cut through the kettles," Jason said. "It's faster. And there's more cover."

"What're you expecting? An air attack?" Cam said, wondering what the kettles were, but afraid to ask.

"Very funny." Jason veered uphill behind the archery range and was swallowed by the pines.

"Cripes—that—guy—can—move," Whaler panted. He paused at the crossroads of two dirt paths, both of which led deeper into the woods. "You know where he's taking us?"

"The kettles," Cam said.

"Oh. Yeah." From Whaler's blank expression, Cam figured he didn't know anything about the strange-sounding place either. "I hope he doesn't go off and leave us," Whaler said. "I'm lost already."

"Stick with me." Cam indicated the right fork in the path. "He can't be that far ahead." They tramped on in silence for several minutes. "There!" Cam pointed to a blur of foliage. "See him?"

"Hey, Jason!" Whaler hollered. "Wait up!"

The blur refocused into a shirt, a pair of pants. As Jason doubled back, his image loomed larger. His mouth and eyes were like angry scars. "What do you guys think you're doing, huh?" His breath was moist and stale. "You want everyone to know where we are?"

Cam shook his head; it was what Jason would expect. But inside, laughter fizzed like 7UP. He tightened his belt around Jason's pants, then bent over to reroll the cuffs so that they were snug around his ankles. The whole thing was ridiculous. They didn't even have any spoils for the other teams to take. What was the big deal?

Cam glanced over at Whaler, who seemed shorter by six inches in the wake of Jason's ire. "Sorry," Whaler mumbled. "Guess we weren't thinking."

"Guess not," Jason said. He hugged himself as if he were cold, which was weird, given the heat. "Come on. Let's go back."

"But I thought you said—" Cam broke off, patted down Jason's torso. Something square and bony was hidden beneath his shirt. "You found something? Already? What is it?"

Jason scouted the area, then pulled Cam and Whaler off the trail, deeper into the woods. Pine boughs slapped Cam's face, brushed back his hair. A carpet of brown needles crunched beneath his feet, then rolled away sharply. Cam hesitated at the rim of a bowl-shaped dip in the landscape. Jason slid down the side, with Whaler at his heels. He motioned Cam impatiently.

"What's this? A bomb crater?" Cam said.

"Shhh!" Whaler and Jason hissed in unison.

Cam scooted down the incline. "Well, are you going to tell me?"

"You've got war on the brain," Jason said. "We're in the kettles, remember?"

"Yeah, so?"

"Ever heard of glaciers? Ever heard of kettle moraines?" Jason said. "Jeez, Cam, you're slipping."

Cam smiled weakly. He had to watch himself, keep his mouth shut like Whaler did. Let Jason think he was with him all the way.

"Are you going to show us what you found or not?" Whaler said.

Jason craned his neck to scout the higher ground. "Not here," he whispered. "Anyone could see us." He charged up the other side of the hollow and ducked again into the woods.

"Oh, give me a break," Cam muttered under his breath. His feet slipped out from under him as he struggled for a handhold. Whaler boosted him from behind. "This better be good."

"Knowing Jason," Whaler said, "it will be."

Somewhere behind them, a twig snapped. Cam dove for cover in the woods, flattened himself against the ground, his heartbeat in his ears. He sensed Whaler, panting at his heels. Had they been followed? Where was Jason? He ventured a look over his shoulder, saw only Whaler.

"Good reflexes, guys. Now you're getting the idea." Jason circled toward them from the other side of the kettle. Cam checked the anger that boiled up without warning. It's just a joke. Lighten up.

"Darn near gave me a heart attack," Whaler said, struggling to his feet.

"Never fear. I know CPR." Jason plunked himself down beside Cam and began unbuttoning his shirt. "Here. You want to see?"

Cam drew his legs to his chest and drank in the shade's delicious coolness. He watched with interest as Jason withdrew a strange metal contraption. "What in the world is that?" he asked.

"Squirrel trap," Jason said.

Whaler examined it, then shook his head. "Nope. That's a one-ten Conibear. Raccoons."

Jason raised one eyebrow. "Whoa. Excuse me."

"Looks more like a giant Chinese puzzle trick if you ask me," Cam said.

Jason laughed. "Whatever. It still beats a rusty old can. We're off to a good start, don't you think?"

"Great," Cam said. "Now all we have to do is get it back to main camp before the bell rings without getting caught."

"Yeah." Whaler nodded glumly. "Think we'll make it?"

"Ask me no questions, I'll tell you no lies," Jason said in a singsongy voice, and winked mysteriously as he slipped the trap back inside his shirt. "Follow me." He wove among the trees, emerging at last just uphill from the archery range. "Get down!" He pointed to a cluster of boys by the equipment shed.

Cam crouched behind a clump of wild carrots and waited for Jason's all-clear signal. But instead of standing up, Jason began belly-crawling toward the shed. He motioned for Whaler and Cam to follow suit.

Cam rolled his eyes. Jason was acting as if this were basic training. The whole thing was ridiculous. Why couldn't they just wait until the other boys had gone? Cam thought fleetingly about standing up and outright walking, but decided it wasn't worth making Jason mad again. Besides, they'd kill him if he made them lose the trap to another team; it *was* a great find. What the heck? he thought, and snaked through the weeds after the others.

The incline ended in a rock retaining-wall. After the boys near the shed had moved on, Jason dropped over the edge and inspected the individual rocks. "Whaler," he said, "stand guard. Let me know if anyone's coming."

"You got it."

Jason continued his inspection, until at last he fixed on a reddish boulder at the base of the wall. "Good! It's still here. Help me, Cam," he said, struggling to move it.

Cam imagined the headline: TWO BOYS BURIED IN ROCKSLIDE, followed by a quote from his father: "We only wanted him to have some fun," said a grief-stricken Alan Whitney, professor of ag-journalism at the University of Wisconsin. "He wanted to go to Interlochen. If only we'd let him, he'd be alive today."

"Cam!" Jason snapped. "Hurry up!"

Cam grasped the rock and helped inch it outward. To his surprise, a small burrow appeared. Jason hurriedly slipped the trap from beneath his shirt and tossed it into the hiding place. "Let's close 'er up," he said.

The rock back in place, they headed over to Olympus. As the activity bell signaled the end of the session, Cam heaved a sigh of relief. At least we won't have to worry about an ambush, he thought. At least the dumb game's over for today.

Through swimming lessons and lunch, archery and dinner, Cam blended in, went with the flow. Maybe he'd made the right decision in playing the game. He, Jason, and Whaler were really getting close—so close that when Jason's parents didn't call to wish him a happy birthday, it was Cam and Whaler who convinced Pee Wee to make a run into town just before taps to pick up an ice-cream cake. Despite the last-minute celebration, Cam felt sorry for Jason, whose grinning good humor never quite managed to mask his disappointment.

Now, as Cam awaited his tentmates' soft snoring, his watch face glowed green beneath the covers. Ten-thirty. Soon. Soon.

Buddy tossed and muttered. Cam couldn't tell whether he was asleep or merely trying to get comfortable. At last Pee Wee shone his flashlight on each boy in turn, then whispered to Cam, "All set? I think the coast is clear."

"What about Buddy?"

Pee Wee checked again. "Sound asleep."

"You're sure?"

"See for yourself," Pee Wee said. "I'll hold the light."

Cam crawled to the end of his bed and peered closely at Buddy. Buddy's mouth, sagging partially open, was softer in slumber. With his hair splayed out on his pillow, the purple scar above his eye stood out in relief.

"Satisfied?" Pee Wee whispered.

Cam nodded. He slid his backpack from under his bed, pulled his sneakers and windbreaker on, and tiptoed across the floor. Buddy snorted in his sleep, freezing Cam in the open doorway. "No! Don't!" Buddy's cry was choked, childlike.

Cam clutched his backpack to his chest. His heart beat faster. Pee Wee bent over Buddy for a long moment, then motioned for Cam to go. The moon was just a silver sliver in the sky. Forest night sounds pulsed around him. Was Buddy really asleep? he wondered. Or had it all been an act?

At last Pee Wee joined him outside. "It was just a bad dream," he whispered. "Go on up. If you need me, I'll be over at Mountain Man's. Last-ditch Fourth of July party. You understand."

Cam nodded and took off for the lodge. Satisfied that the rec room was deserted, he closed the door, turned up the lights, and assembled his flute. Maybe this would work after all. Especially if he could catch a quick nap every afternoon. He flew through his warm-ups, eager to begin the Mozart.

The notes echoed through the tomblike hall. Cam winced at a shrill mistake, and restudied the measure.

He could master the piece *now,* not in the fall. All this baloney about hitting a plateau was simply mind over matter. Hadn't Dad always said, "You can do anything you set your mind to, Cam?" And hadn't Cam found a way to practice? It was true then. Of course it was. Mrs. Ellison meant well, but she was mistaken. Cam began again, and struggled to clean up the passage. Not exactly on par with Jean-Pierre Rampal, he thought. But he'd get there. He had time.

A sudden draft blew past him. Goose bumps scuttled down his arms. He'd closed the door, hadn't he? Of course he had. There was no way he'd risk being discovered. Even so, he felt a presence, unseen eyes trained in his direction, and scanned the room. Don't be ridiculous. There's no one here. He pressed his lips against the instrument. A kind of shuffling sound drifted toward him from the rack of folding chairs across the room. His heart beat like a metronome cranked up to 192.

FIVE

REFLEXIVELY, CAM SLIPPED his flute up his sleeve, cradled the end in his palm. A dumb move when he considered that he was standing there with all the lights on. "Who . . . who's there?" he said.

No one replied. Cam's echo bounced back like an owl's cry: *Who? Who?* He was just imagining things. But what about that draft? Better not take any chances. That's enough for tonight, he thought, easing the instrument out of hiding.

Unable to shake the feeling that he was being watched, his hands were trembling as he disassembled the flute and reamed the handkerchief through each joint.

"What's the big hurry?" Buddy strolled out of the

shadows, a sardonic smile wrinkling his face. "Don't leave on my account."

Words caught in Cam's throat. He was fumbling with the head joint now, trying to fit it into its contoured slot in the case. But it was upside-down. Backward. Stupid, because he'd done it a million times, could do it with his eyes closed.

"A flute, huh?" Buddy said. He gave Cam a limp-wristed wave. "Only girls play flute. No wonder you're hiding out in here."

Cam scowled. "Not true. Ever heard of James Galway? Jean-Pierre Rampal?"

"Jean-Pierre?" Buddy batted his lashes. "Sweet name."

Cam said nothing. What good would it do, arguing with an idiot? He just had to get out of here and the worst would be over. Unthreading the handkerchief, he slipped the metal prod into the case, then snapped it shut. As he stuffed the flute and music into his back-pack, his worry eased. So what if Buddy teased him? It wasn't the end of the world. At least Buddy hadn't touched anything. Cam shuddered at the thought. When he looked up, Buddy was shaking his head.

"I don't get it. Your folks are never gonna know if you don't practice. What've they got on you anyway?"

"Nothing," Cam said. "It's not like that."

"Yeah? Nobody practices cuz they want to."

"Shows what you know," Cam muttered.

"What was that?"

"Nothing. I just said 'I know.' " Cam jerked his backpack off the Ping-Pong table.

Buddy seized his wrist. "I'll take that," he said, wresting the pack from Cam's hand.

"No, that's okay." Cam feigned nonchalance, though his heart was throbbing in his chest. "I can do it."

Buddy's laugh bounced off the walls, landed in Cam's ears like well-placed blows. For a moment, he was too stunned to react. Then he flung himself at Buddy, only to be stopped by Buddy's outstretched arm.

"Look," Buddy said, "I'll make you a deal."

"No deals. Give it back or I'll tell Pee Wee."

Cam cursed himself for saying that he would snitch. He'd never win Buddy over *that* way. He may as well have waved a red flag in front of a mad bull.

"Don't even think about ratting," Buddy said. "That is, unless you want to go flute fishing on the bottom of the lake."

Cam backed off. "You wouldn't do that. I know you wouldn't."

"Oh, no? You wanna make a bet?" Buddy encased the backpack in his arms, inclining his chin defiantly.

"Come on now. This isn't funny."

"I didn't say it was," Buddy replied. "I'm serious. *Now* are you gonna listen?" Cam swallowed hard and nodded. "The deal is, you're gonna spy for me and Mick."

"Spy?" Cam said, his voice cracking. "On who?"

"Jason and Whaler. Who else?"

"And you'll give me back my flute?"

"I didn't say that," Buddy said, smirking.

"Then there's no deal. Why should I spy for you?"

"You *do* want your little flutey-pie to be safe, don't you?" Buddy patted the pack as if he were burping a baby. "I promise I'll take real good care of it, as long as you give us what we want."

"But . . ."

"Think fast, gook. Lake's not very far. And this baby'd sink like a stone." His unflinching gaze held no hint of amusement.

"You do it," Cam said, "and they'll send you back home."

"So what?" Buddy snapped. "Maybe I wanna go home. Something wrong with that?" Cam shook his head quickly. If Buddy didn't care about the consequences, maybe he *would* carry out his threat. "Okay, then. What's it gonna be?"

"You promise you'll take care of it?" Cam said.

"I told you I would." Buddy grated his ID tag back and forth along its chain. "So?"

Cam avoided Buddy's snake-eye, as if looking into it might hypnotize him. Instead, he stared at his backpack. The thought of entrusting it to Buddy turned Cam's stomach, and for a crazy moment he thought he might have an attack of diarrhea. There was no way he could risk Buddy's making good his threat. Next to his parents, he realized, he loved that flute more than anything. Himself included. And he'd do whatever it took to keep it safe—even spy on his friends. "Okay," he sighed. "What do you want to know?"

"There you go. That wasn't hard, was it?" Buddy slapped him on the back, and Cam cringed. "So, tell me what you guys found."

"Nothing much. Just a trap or something." A lizard darted out from under the rack of chairs and stared up at Cam reproachfully before scurrying off into the lavatory. Wouldn't it be just like Buddy to use a slime-ball lizard to heap on the guilt? He'd probably trained it and planted it there himself just to turn the screws.

"What do you mean, trap?" Buddy prodded. "Like a bear trap?"

"I don't know." Cam shrugged. "Yeah, I guess. A Caught-A-Bear Whaler called it."

"You mean Conibear," Buddy said. "What size?"

"How should I know?" Cam hugged himself and massaged away the goose bumps that were crawling up and down his arms beneath his windbreaker. "Can I go now?"

"In a minute," Buddy said. "First tell me where it is."

"No way. Those guys'd kill me."

Buddy just shrugged and began unzipping the backpack. "Suit yourself. It's your flute." He pulled out the case, unfastened it, and stroked the instrument with mock affection. Cam swallowed hard, blinked quickly. Buddy smiled. "Last one to the lake is a rotten—"

"Okay! I'll tell."

"Good." As Buddy put the flute away, Cam unballed his fists. "See? A promise is a promise. You remember that."

Cam nodded. So what if Buddy and Mick got their

hands on the trap? It was just a game, right? Part of the tactics. As long as his flute was safe, he didn't care what they did. "You know the rock wall behind the archery shed?" he said at last.

"Yeah, so?"

"Check behind the reddish rock." As Cam started toward the door, he looked over his shoulder at his backpack nestling in Buddy's arms. Now how am I going to practice? He gulped down the lump in his throat. His eyes watered and he blinked quickly. "You coming?"

"Sure," Buddy said, shouldering the backpack. "Why not? I got what I came for."

Yeah, a spy, Cam thought. You got what you came for all right.

The next day's Spoils of War session was held after lunch. "Let's hit the campground first thing," Jason said. "I'll bet we make a haul."

"Us and everyone else." Whaler folded the letter he'd been reading and stuffed it in his pocket. "The trap's cool. Why don't we just quit while we're ahead? Make everyone think we don't have anything to take."

Cam wondered whether guilt had a smell. Any second, he imagined, Jason and Whaler would stare at him oddly, then sniff out his dirty secret. I'm a spy. Cam could hardly believe it himself. But he had no choice. He *had* to play along, didn't he?

"You're awfully quiet," Jason said as they passed the

archery range. It sounded more like an accusation than an observation.

Cam beat down the impulse to defend himself. He had to keep it light and friendly, as if nothing had changed. Had to remember who his true friends were. "Yeah," Cam said. "I guess I *am* kind of quiet, aren't I?"

"Wanna read my letter?" Whaler said. "It's from my little sister. Guaranteed to make you smile."

"Thanks anyway." Cam glanced at the reddish rock in the wall behind the shed. From this distance it was impossible to tell whether Buddy had raided their hiding place yet. If not, it was just a matter of time. And Cam didn't want to be there when Jason pulled out the stone. He quickened his pace and charged up the hill.

To his left sprawled the Swamp, a marshy, overgrown area teeming with insects; and beyond it lay Rainbow Lake. Cam paused to admire the view as much as to catch his breath. The sun glinted off aluminum canoes and rowboats, tossed haphazardly across the lake like so many jacks from a gigantic, unseen hand. A baseball diamond, parched and deserted, hugged the Swamp's western edge. Whaler paused beside Cam, his chest heaving. He caught Cam's eye and smiled his thanks for the chance to catch his breath.

"Come on, girls," Jason said. "Let's get the lead out, shall we?"

At the main campfire ring, they cut left, away from the kettles. A team of younger campers popped out of the woods, blocking their way. "We got you!" a freckle-faced kid said, tagging Jason's arm. "Give us your spoils."

"Sorry, guys. You're S.O.L.," Jason said, winking at Cam.

"Huh?"

"Sure out of luck," Cam cut in, before Jason could use the real S-word. "We don't have anything." *On us, anyway. And maybe not even in our hiding place either.* He nudged aside a twinge of guilt over lying to their captors. *First a spy, now a liar. What next?* he wondered.

The boys looked unconvinced and held fast to Jason's arm.

"Go ahead," Whaler said. "You wanna search us?"

They stared up at Whaler, his arms crossed over his massive chest, and shook their heads. Then, with a collective sigh of exasperation, they took off toward the kettles.

"One of the benefits of having a hiding place," Jason said. "Believe me, you learn these things after a few summers. Come on, before the whole campground is crawling with guys." He veered from the path and into the scrub oak woods, dodging for cover behind a hedge of wild honeysuckle.

Cam and Whaler hustled after him, following his lead. At last, the outline of several RVs broke through the monotonous campground landscape.

"We need someone to be lookout." Jason glanced from Whaler to Cam.

"I'll do it," Cam said. Too quickly. He could tell by the way Jason's eyebrows practically shot off his face. "I mean, I will, if no one else wants to."

"Whaler?"

"Let Cam. Maybe someone will throw us an extra hot dog or something. I'm starving."

"Just whistle if you see anyone. Especially Fiedler."

"Right," Cam said. Being lookout. The perfect cover if Buddy and Mick should come along and start pumping him for information. At least they wouldn't be overheard.

"What's the matter?" Jason said. "Aren't you gonna wish us good luck?"

"Oh." Cam shook free of his thoughts, accepted another stab of guilt. "Sure. Yeah. Good luck."

To Cam's relief, no one came by. Soon Whaler and Jason returned with an assortment of junk—some old rags and tin cans, an empty wine bottle, wads of tinfoil, and a lighter-fluid container.

"Is that empty?" Cam asked.

Jason shook the can. "Almost. But don't worry. The cap's wedged on so tight, this stuff isn't going anywhere."

"What good is it?" Cam said. "I think you should just throw it away."

"Are you kidding?" Whaler said. "Someone throws a cigarette in there and—"

"Kablooey!" Jason pantomimed an explosion, and Cam jumped at the sudden circling of his arms. Jason redeemed himself with an impish grin. "Whaler's right," he said. "It's too dangerous, throwing it away. Here. Help us hide 'em till we get back to the rock."

Cam stuffed a couple of rags in his pockets and hid the wine bottle inside his shirt while Jason wedged the can of lighter fluid into the back of Whaler's pants, covering it with Whaler's shirttail. "Don't anybody light a match," Whaler said.

"Why? Did you fart?" Jason's eyes glinted.

"Very funny," Cam said.

Whaler regarded him with mock horror. "No it's not."

"Cut it out, you two," Jason said. "Let's go unload this stuff before we get caught."

Unload, Cam thought. As in hide. He dogged after the others, half wishing Buddy and Mick would ambush them along the way. At least that would take away their reason for going to the rock. And it would save Cam's having to tell Buddy later what they'd found. But, except for a couple of squirrels that skittered out of their path, they encountered nothing.

On the hill above the Swamp, Jason signaled a halt. He pulled out a wad of foil and juggled it from hand to hand. "Enemy spotted at nine o'clock," he intoned. "Request permission to pull the pin."

"I don't see anyone." Cam scowled.

Whaler parted the high-standing weeds and pointed to two figures below them on the ball diamond. They might have been Buddy and Mick, or any other two guys with blond hair. "Permission granted, sir," Whaler said.

Jason made a big deal of pulling an imaginary pin, then hurled the silver ball as if it were a grenade. It arced over the dense foliage and dropped out of sight amid Jason and Whaler's raucous sound effects.

Cam shook his head. "Don't blame me if we get caught," he said. "You guys are making all the noise."

Jason's attempt to stifle his laughter brought a barrage of playful punches from Whaler.

"I'm not kidding," Cam said.

"I'm not kidding," Jason mimicked. "Jeez! Look who's turning into Rambo."

"I am not." Cam pulled out the spoils he'd been hiding. "Here. Take them, if that's the way you want to be."

He shoved the rags and the bottle at Whaler, then bolted for the path. The best defense is a good offense. Who'd said that anyhow? His gym teacher? Who cared, as long as it worked. If the trap *was* missing, they couldn't blame Cam. Hadn't they just seen how serious he was about protecting their loot? No, they wouldn't blame him.

Footsteps pummeled the hardened ground behind him. Whaler huffed in Cam's ear as he plucked him back by the shirt. "Hey," he said, "don't cut out. We were just goofing around."

"Yeah, we're sorry. Come on. Lighten up, man." Jason pressed his hands together as if in prayer, his mischievous eyes full of mock pleading.

A repentant Jason was too funny to stone-face, and

Cam's laughter tumbled out uncensored. "Don't sprain your fingers, Jase." It'll be all right, he thought. We *are* friends, see?

"Me? Sprain my fingers?" Jason grinned. "Wouldn't think of it."

They continued down the path, past the Swamp to the archery range. The bell tolled from main camp in short, frenzied clangs. Thank goodness. The game was over. At least for now. "Maybe we should just toss this stuff and go," Cam said, indicating the metal barrel near the shed.

Whaler shook his head. "No way. The coast is clear. I say we stash it."

"Yeah," Jason said. "Never know what might impress the judges."

Cam licked his lips and glanced about quickly. "Well, hurry up. I'll stand guard." No sense being right in Jason's face when he pulls back the rock. Relieved that neither Jason nor Whaler seemed to notice his eagerness, Cam hid behind the shed and peered around the corner. As Jason and Whaler puffed to move the rock, his heart shifted gears.

"What the . . . ?" Jason did not finish. Did not need to. Cam knew exactly what he was talking about.

"Let me see," Whaler said. There was silence, except for Cam's heartbeat, which churned in his ears like helicopter blades. Whaler uttered a single curse.

"Wh-what is it?" Cam called over his shoulder. He braced himself for accusations, but none came. "What's wrong?"

"Come look at this," Jason said, his voice heavy with disgust. "We've been had."

Cam closed his eyes before turning toward them, and prayed quickly for the right face, the right words. Then he hurried from the shed's safety to gawk at the empty cache. He let his jaw sag open, added a curse of his own. Jason's eyes bored holes into Cam's forehead, and Cam could not look up.

"It had to be Buddy and Mick," Jason said at last. "But how?"

"Search me." Cam shook his head, tried to muster more conviction in his voice. "Really, guys," he said. "I don't know."

SIX

CAM'S CHEEKS BURNED under his friends' scrutiny. "Maybe it *wasn't* Buddy," he said. "Did you ever think of that? Maybe some other team saw us yesterday. Or somebody from last summer knew about the—"

"Could be," Jason cut in, "but I doubt it. Anyone else besides Buddy would play by the rules."

"Yeah." Whaler dusted his hands on his jeans. "Think we should make our own trap? Catch 'em in the act?"

Jason looked up at Whaler in surprise. "Brilliant idea, Wainwright, if I do say so myself."

Cam mumbled similar praise and Whaler grinned sheepishly. Jason stared off toward the Swamp. Cam wondered what Jason could be plotting, but his expression held no clue. When at last he turned searching eyes on Cam, Cam writhed under the examination.

"What's the matter with you?" Jason said.

Cam hugged himself to muffle the pounding in his chest. "Nothing. It just gives me the creeps is all, wondering if Big Buddy is watching us."

"Yeah." Jason's chuckle made Cam feel as if he were off the hook—for the moment, anyway. "I know just what you mean."

They don't suspect me! Cam's tension relaxed its viselike hold on his body. Like he'd said, anyone could have found their hiding place; there didn't *have* to be a traitor.

"What are we going to do with all this stuff?" Whaler said. "Can't very well hide it here anymore."

"Not all of it anyway." Jason smiled mysteriously.

"What's that supposed to mean?" Cam asked.

Jason patted the air, signaling patience. "All part of the plan. You *do* want us to catch 'em in the act, don't you?" Cam bobbed his head. "Well, then," Jason continued, "what we need first is a spy."

Spy! The word screamed in Cam's ears. He swallowed hard, glanced over at Whaler.

Whaler was backing away, covering his face with his hands as if to avoid having his picture taken. "Don't look at me, man," he said. "No way I want to mess with those two."

If I spied on Buddy, I'd have an excuse to talk to him, Cam thought. And Jason wouldn't get suspicious, seeing us together. "I'll do it," he said, lest Jason himself volunteer.

"You?" Jason's eyes narrowed. "What's the deal?"

Cam shrugged. "I just want to help, that's all." Cameron Whitney, double agent. His legs turned to cooked spaghetti at the thought. He steeled himself against Jason's hard stare. What was that about anyway? Did Jason want to be the spy? "Look," Cam said, "if *you* want to do it, fine."

"No, no." Jason smiled. "You be the spy. That'll be perfect."

"I don't get what you want me to do."

"Me either," Whaler said. "Those guys aren't going to let Cam anywhere near them. So what's he supposed to spy on?"

Jason fell silent, twitching his mouth from one side to the other. "Maybe spy's the wrong word," he said at last. "I think what we need is a traitor."

"A traitor?" Cam's voice cracked on the word.

"Yeah, you know," Whaler chimed in. "Convince them you're mad at us, that you want to change sides, only you don't really."

That would be perfect! Cam squelched the impulse to agree without protest. "But they don't even like me," he said. "Why should they believe anything I say?"

"Because you'll give them information." Jason's eyes gleamed. "Of course, we'll tell you *what* information."

Cam's whole body breathed a sigh of relief. He could not believe his luck. Who would have thought that being a double spy could work out just fine? "Great!" he said. "When do I get started?"

"No time like the present." Jason tossed the lighter-fluid can into the hiding place. "Here. Help me with the rock."

Cam did, then dusted off his hands. Scowling at the gritty residue, he rinsed them in the water fountain beside the equipment shed. "Isn't burying that stuff kind of dangerous?" he asked.

"Nah." Jason waved away his concern. "By my calculations, it'll be out of there within the hour."

"But what do I—"

"Just let it slip what we found," Jason said. "Only don't tell them where we hid it, okay?"

"Yeah, and we'll be here waiting when they make their move, right?" Jason nodded, and Whaler clapped a big hand on Cam's back. "It's a tough job," Whaler continued, "but someone's got to do it."

"And better me than you, right?" Cam teased. Then, with a carefree wave to his teammates—my friends, he reminded himself—he started off toward the playing field in search of Buddy and Mick.

"Remember," Jason called after him, "don't tell them where it is. And don't forget what side you're on."

Cam flashed a thumbs-up sign in the air but did not turn back to look at them again. Dry grass crunched beneath his feet as he crossed the field. He wouldn't forget what side he was on; that was the last thing he'd do. He knew who his friends were; Jason and Whaler needed have no fear about that. Two blond heads towered above a group of boys gathered near the backstop.

As he hurried toward them, Cam rehearsed what he'd say to Buddy and Mick: "We found lighter fluid. You know where to find it."

So what if Jason and Whaler caught those two in the act? What were they going to do? Hand-to-hand combat? Unlikely. And Buddy wouldn't rat on Cam because then he'd lose his spy. What was the worst that could happen? Cam wondered. Mick and Buddy would have the lighter fluid, and Whaler and Jason would be mad. That was it. No big deal. He could live with that.

As he neared the knot of campers, Mick called out a greeting. "You come to rescue us?"

As he drew closer, Cam could see that the younger boys were clutching Mick and Buddy's clothes, holding them prisoner. "They won't give us their spoils," one kid complained. "We caught them fair and square. Before the bell rang, too. Go get a counselor, will you?"

Cam could feel his face melt into a wide grin. Ah, Buddy, let 'em have it, whatever it is, he thought. Give 'em a break.

"*You* guys were supposed to catch us," Buddy hissed, tossing his head. "Not these wimps. Go get Jason. You can even tell him where we hid our stuff."

"Not fair!"

"Tell us! We caught you first!"

Buddy's being generous? Cam felt a nudge of suspicion. "I don't *know* where you hid your stuff," Cam said. "And even if I did, why should I tell Jason?"

Buddy strained against his captors but the kids tightened their grip on his belt. "Because," he said, "you want a certain item to be safe, remember?"

Cam gulped. His flute. What with all this double spy nonsense, he'd almost forgotten. "I remember," he said glumly.

"Tell him to look near that old dead tree at the edge of the Swamp," Buddy said. "And hurry, will you? These kids are getting on my nerves."

Cam hesitated, uncertain what he would be leading Jason into. Remember whose side you are on. Yeah, right. He might as well deliver his team's message now. "Don't you want to hear what *we* found?" he asked Buddy.

"Yeah, sure." Buddy winked at Mick. "Kid's a fast learner."

Cam eyed the younger campers. They were about to witness his little spy mission, and telling them was definitely *not* part of the deal. "R-E-T-H-G-I-L," he said pointedly. "D-I-U-L-F."

"What?" Buddy bristled with annoyance.

"Do it again," Mick said. "I only got part of it." Cam repeated the backward spelling. Mick's eyes grew wide. "You putting us on?" Cam shook his head.

"What is it, man?" Buddy said, glaring at Cam. Mick leaned over and whispered into Buddy's ear. A grin transformed the thinner boy's face. "All right! Where?"

Cam measured his words, hoping to protect the younger boys. The last thing he wanted was some little kid getting caught in the middle of Jason and Buddy's stupid war. For all he knew, maybe one of them had been bright enough to crack his code. "Oh," he said offhandedly, "I think you know where."

"Right," Buddy said. He tried again to shake the minicampers loose, but they clung even tighter. "Go get Lowman, man. I mean it. I've had it with these little leeches."

One of the smallest kids released his grip on Mick's leg. His mouth stretched into a pout. "I am not a leech," he said, his fists drilled into his hips. "You guys think you're so big."

"No we don't," Mick said. "We just don't want—" Buddy glared at him, and he swallowed the rest of his sentence. "Hurry up, will you?" he said to Cam. There was something in Mick's eyes, a soft pleading, that Cam did not understand. Yet he knew that for whatever reason, it was important that he go get Jason. Fast.

With Buddy and Mick still wriggling to free themselves from their captors, he bolted across the playing field. The smallest boy tagged after him for a while, then lost ground. When Cam turned back, the kid was heading toward the old dead tree at the edge of the Swamp. Buddy hollered something that Cam could not understand, and Cam quickened his pace. At last, breathless, he reached the rock retaining-wall behind the shed.

"Jason! Whaler! Get out here," he said. "I don't know why, but Buddy says you've got to come quick." He scanned the clearing, but there was no sign of his friends. Where could they have gone? "You guys! I told them. You can come out now."

The door to the archery shed creaked behind him. He whirled about to face Jason and Whaler. "God, why don't you tell the whole world?" Jason said, his tone like a saber. "What's the matter with you anyway?"

Cam mumbled an apology. "But there's nobody around," he said, "and besides, Buddy and Mick aren't coming."

"Why not?" Jason demanded. "Didn't you set the bait?"

"Of course I did." Cam mustered an indignant stance. "They *can't* come. Some kids have got them."

"All right!" When Whaler held up his hand to high-five Jason, Jason just glared at them both. Whaler shoved his hands into his pockets and hiked up his shoulders, avoiding Jason's eyes.

"Rats! The whole plan's wrecked now. Somehow we've got to free them, so they can come sniffing around."

"Don't look at me," Whaler said. "Let Cam do it. Yeah!" His dark eyes caught Jason's usual spark. "That way he can convince them he's on *their* side."

"Great! I bet that'll work!" Jason offered a high five of his own, and Whaler beamed like a kid who had just redeemed himself in his father's eyes. "Okay, Cam, my man, it's up to you."

"How am I supposed to free them from eight kids?" He blew out his exasperation, and looked from Jason to Whaler. They did not reply. "Look," Cam said, "I thought we were a team. You guys have to help, too. Why don't you just *pretend* to go where they want you to? Create a diversion—isn't that what you call it?"

Jason grinned and squeezed Cam's shoulder. "Jeez, settle down. You act like we're throwing you to the wolves."

"If the shoe fits," Cam said. His mother's expression flew to his lips. A sudden pang of homesickness rose in his chest. If only Mom could see him now, trapped in this stupid game. She'd have to realize that Camp Rainbow Lake had been a mistake. A big one. And of course she'd convince his father; she could be Cam's greatest ally when she felt he was being mistreated. No way Professor Diane Whitney would ever be accused of not trying to protect her only child from life's messy moments. The problem was, she could be downright shrill and embarrassing, so Cam usually kept these little incidents to himself just to avoid Mom's creating a scene. Right now, though, he'd welcome her interference with open arms. . . .

"He's got a point," Whaler was saying. "After all, we *are* a team."

"So where are we supposed to go?" Jason said. "I bet it's a trick. I can feel it in my bones."

As Cam repeated Buddy's directions, he remembered the pleading look in Mick's eyes, remembered the little kid heading off toward the Swamp. "I don't know about that," Cam said, "but I think you'd better hurry."

Jason rolled his eyes skyward. "Yeah, yeah. I'm going. You just get the kids to release Buddy and Mick. Then we'll circle back." He took off at a trot and was quickly outdistanced by Whaler's longer strides.

Cam sighed. So far, so good. He'd convinced Jason to do what Buddy wanted; his flute would be safe, at least for a while. Once again he jogged across the field. All this running was sure to help his breath control—if Buddy ever decided to let him practice again.

"All right," he said to the others, "Jason and Whaler are on their way."

"Too late, Cam."

"Is not," Buddy snapped. "They'll find it."

"Find what?" Cam said.

Neither Buddy nor Mick answered, but the glance they exchanged sent a chill down Cam's spine. He nudged the younger campers, tried to unpeel their fingers from the taller boys' belts.

"Whatever it is, Joey's gonna find it first," one kid said. "Just you wait."

A high-pitched scream shot out of the Swamp. Was it real or some kind of trick? Cam whirled about, strained to hear it again. There! It *was* a scream but he couldn't tell whose. Dread hobbled him like leg irons as he sped toward the old dead tree, the pack of kids at his heels.

SEVEN

JASON CRASHED OUT of the Swamp, beating gnats away from his face. "Good job, man," he said as he brushed past Cam. "Look at 'em. They're making a run for the shed. Just like I thought."

Cam refused to look. How could Jason care about Buddy and Mick at a time like this? "W-what happened in there?" he asked. "Who screamed?"

"Search me." Jason shrugged. "Ask Whaler. Catch you later, okay?" He stole along the edge of the Swamp, his camouflage clothes fading into the overgrowth.

As the younger boys propelled Cam forward, the ground changed, became moist and oozy despite the drought. The tree ahead loomed like a great, gray claw against the sky. He could hear Whaler's voice, calm and masterful, above a child's moans.

"Move back," Whaler said. "Give him room." The other boys obeyed. Cam edged closer, unable to see beyond Whaler, who knelt beside an apparently injured boy. "There, there. It's gonna be okay. Betcha it's just a bad bruise. Here. Let me see."

"Whaler, it's me. What happened?"

Whaler looked up briefly, then turned his attention back to the boy. "Got caught. In a trap," he said. "A one-ten Conibear. Funny thing about that."

"God." The word escaped Cam like a prayer rather than a curse. Peering over Whaler's shoulder, Cam could see now that the injured boy was Joey. Color seemed to drain from beneath Joey's tan, and his eyes clung to Whaler's as if an invisible lifeline connected him to the older boy. "What should I do?" Cam asked. "Is he going to be okay?"

"Yes, he's going to be just fine." Whaler crooned directly to Joey, cradling the boy in his arms. "Happened to my brother once and alls he got was a bad bruise. Come on," he said to Joey. "Let's get you up to the nurse."

Cam shooed the other boys away as Whaler stood up slowly. Though small sobs shook Joey's chest, he was no longer moaning. Whaler kicked the trap aside. "Get that thing out of here," he said under his breath to Cam, "before it causes any more trouble."

"Right." Cam retrieved the trap and hid it beneath his shirt. "This was meant for Jason, you know."

Whaler nodded. "Come on, Joey. Put your arms around my neck now. That's right. We'll get some ice on it, okay? We'll make it all better. That's a boy."

Cam slogged after Whaler, a hard knot growing in his throat. This was all his fault. If he hadn't told Buddy about the trap, none of this would have happened. But what else could he have done? Cam was certain that Buddy would have destroyed his flute if he told Pee Wee or refused to cooperate. No, there was nothing else he could have done. Besides, who would have thought that Buddy would go and set the dumb thing?

Back on parched grass again, Cam wiped the muck off his sneakers, then pressed on toward main camp. They'd created a diversion all right. By now Mick and Buddy were probably off stealing the lighter fluid. And Jason would be getting his jollies, spying on them from the woods or the equipment shed. Let them do their thing, he thought. What do I care?

The younger boys had run ahead to find their counselor and tell him about Joey. Sweat beaded on Whaler's forehead and trickled down his neck as he took the last hill. His steady, soothing assurances to the injured boy were like rainfall. "You really miss your brother, don't you, Whaler?" Cam said.

"Brother*s*," he corrected. "And sisters. Shows, huh?"

Cam nodded. "Bet they miss you too."

"Wasn't *my* choice to come here," Whaler said. "But I couldn't hurt my folks' feelings. They were so happy they could spring me loose from babysitting and send me. How could I tell them I'd rather stay home?"

Cam shrugged. He supposed he ought to feel grateful to *his* parents too, but resentment reared its ugly head instead. "I wanted to go to camp all right," he said, "but not at a place like this."

Whaler fell silent. "Well," he said at last, "if my dad gets cut from the team, I'm leaving. I don't care what they say. I want to be there with him, you know?" When Cam said he didn't, Whaler explained that his father played second-string for the Green Bay Packers. "Sam 'Bam' Wainwright. Never heard of him, right?"

"What do I know?" Cam said, sensing Whaler's disappointment. "I don't even know who Burt Starr is."

Whaler laughed. "Try *Bart.* And steer clear of Green Bay."

"Yeah, right." Cam didn't have to be a sports nut to know that the former big-shot quarterback and coach's name was really Bart. But it was worth it, playing dumb, just to get a smile out of Whaler and distract him from worrying about his dad.

The nurse's cabin with its pea green roof poked through the trees. "We're almost there, Joey," Cam said. "Hang tough, okay?" Hypocrite. Who was he to talk about hanging tough? It sounded better, coming from Whaler.

As they mounted the steps to the porch, Cam hung back. He wished he could find somewhere to ditch the trap that he still clutched guiltily beneath his shirt. "Come on, man," Whaler said, "get the door, will you?" Cam did, and Whaler squeezed past him, taking care not to bump Joey's foot against the jamb.

A woman shuffled over to greet them, her limbs pushing like white toothpaste out of her uniform top and cutoff jeans. A long brown braid fell over one shoulder. "Good Lord, what happened here?" she said. "Let me take a look. Which one is it?"

"The left." Whaler eased Joey onto a cot. "Got caught in a trap."

"Oh, my." The nurse blanched. "What did you use to stop the bleeding?"

"Isn't any," Whaler said.

"How could there *not* be?" She regarded Whaler as if he were an idiot or a liar, probably thinking that any self-respecting trap would have steel jaws like in the cartoons. As she set about examining Joey's foot, she seemed genuinely surprised not to find a wound. "You're sure it was a trap? Good Lord! What's a thing like that doing in camp?"

Whaler shifted his weight, telegraphing his uneasiness to Cam. "I—I don't know, ma'am," Cam said, straight-faced. Another lie. He hated how good he was getting at this. His stomach did, too. He'd have to remember to take a couple of Pepto-Bismol tablets. "May we go now? I mean, do you need any more information?"

The nurse blinked at him as if he were an apparition. "What do *you* know about all this?" she said.

Too much, Cam thought. He locked eyes with Whaler and did not reply. Could she see the trap's outline? Could she sniff out his guilt?

"He wasn't even there," Whaler said. "And I came just after it happened. Guess some trapper forgot it is all."

"That right, Joey?" she asked, smoothing back his hair.

His lower lip trembled. "I—I was just trying to find those other guys' spoils," he said. "But"—he looked from the nurse to Whaler—"I wasn't 'posed to go in the Swamp, was I?" His voice was pinched with shame.

"You hush now, and never mind about the Swamp. I've gotta call Mountain Man and take you into town for an X ray. Make sure you'll be good as new in no time."

"Can he come with us?" Joey said, indicating Whaler.

"If he wants to."

"Sure." Whaler smiled. "No problem."

Cam faded back toward the door, feeling like a bit player who'd missed his exit cue. He leaned against the screen and tried to catch Whaler's eye. But his friend had hunkered down beside the cot to await the camp director.

"What's your name anyway?" Joey asked him.

"Jonah," Whaler said without hesitation.

"Gee." Joey's voice was full of wonder. "Like in the Bible, right?"

Cam felt a stab of envy at the way Whaler and Joey were together. Easy, natural. And honest. Everything that Cam was not. At least, not lately. He couldn't bring himself to hang around and hear more. Chucking the trap in the bushes outside the cabin, he wished he could unload his guilt as easily. And was it his imagination, or did the wooden door actually applaud his departure as he hurried down the steps?

Stories about the accident buzzed through camp like a game of Telephone. One version had Joey's leg broken; another had him crippled for life. Cam was relieved when it was time for swimming. At least then he could avoid all the rumors and accusing eyes. Every time guys asked him about the trap, they *were* blaming him, weren't they?

When he stopped by Olympus to change into his swimsuit, Mick was the only one still there. He was stripped down to his shorts. A red rash crept down his arms, across his chest. "At least that Joey kid didn't break anything," he said. "We didn't mean for him to get hurt."

"No. Only Jason."

Mick turned away. "He wouldn't have gotten caught. He's too smart."

Cam said nothing as he whisked his swimsuit off the end of his bunk. Jason *was* smart. But that was no reason to risk setting the trap.

"You get your letter?" Mick asked. "Pee Wee put it on your pillow."

"Thanks." Cam peeled back the envelope flap and pulled out six flimsy pink pages, the first of which he scanned quickly. It was boring, full of chitchat. His mother could write a prize-winning essay on "Nothing Much Happened Since You Left for Camp." He wondered why she bothered. To appease her conscience, probably. Well, Cam thought, she ought to just save herself the stamp. Why couldn't Dad write? He was the one who really shared what was in his heart. Maybe it was the journalist in him. Whatever. There was no putting down one of Dad's letters, that was for sure. Why didn't *he* write? Was he just too busy?

Cam chided himself. He ought to be grateful for Mom's letter. At least she'd written. That was more than Cam had done (although he'd started to—twice). Why did he always freeze up at the sight of a blank page, as if something terrible would happen if he didn't get everything down exactly right? Maybe he'd inherited this quirk from his birth parents—not that it mattered. It was just one of those things he wondered about sometimes, when nothing else explained how different he was from Mom and Dad. But even if he were a fast writer, how could he compose anything meaningful with Buddy and Mick poking around, reading over his shoulder? Maybe it was better to forget about letters altogether and just wait to talk in person.

"From your parents?" Mick asked. Cam nodded. "They coming for Visitors Day?"

"I guess. It's Sunday, right?"

"Yeah." Mick sighed. "Wish I'd hear from home." He hunched his shoulders, then rubbed each arm in succession. His rash looked angrier by the second.

"What've you got? Allergies again?"

"Very funny." Mick forced a smile.

Time for swimming, Cam thought. I should have remembered Mick'd need a new excuse. "I—I wasn't kidding," he said. "That looks gross."

"I know. Doesn't it?" Mick grinned. "Poison ivy. I get it all the time at my grandparents' cabin. S'pose I *should* see the nurse, huh?"

Cam nodded. "But how'd you get it all over your . . ." He broke off, pushed aside the silly thought that popped into his head. No one got poison ivy on purpose. He squinted up at Mick. "You didn't roll in it, did you?"

Mick's Adam's apple bobbed. "So what if I did?" he said. "It worked."

Cam raised his hands. "Hey, it's not *my* body. None of *my* business, right?"

"Right."

"My lips are sealed."

Mick nodded, offered a tentative smile. "Thanks." He rubbed his chest and cringed.

Cam wrinkled up his face. "Better not scratch it. You'll get an infection."

"I know, I know."

"Don't you think it'd be easier to just learn how to swim?"

Mick chuckled. "You might be right. It's just that . . . oh, never mind."

"Whatever," Cam said, eyeing the creeping hives. "I hope it's worth it."

"We all make our choices."

Cam thought about his flute, about his role as a double agent. "Yeah," he said. "I guess we do."

"Well, see you." Mick started toward the door but stopped short of opening it. He turned back and stared at Cam for a long moment. "Look. I don't know what

Buddy's problem is—with you, I mean. But whatever he's got of yours in that backpack—"

"My flute," Cam blurted to his own surprise.

"A flute? Really?"

Cam nodded glumly.

"Well, don't worry," Mick said. "I'll keep an eye on it."

"You will?" Cam's voice climbed a register.

"Yep. Same as I'll keep an eye on the rest of our spoils." Mick winked at Cam; then, scratching his arms and chest, he headed off toward the nurse's.

Cam frowned. What did Mick mean? Could Buddy be keeping their spoils in Cam's backpack, too? With a furtive glance outside the tent, he knelt beside Buddy's bunk and began pawing through his suitcase. Nothing. Where had he hidden the backpack? Cam smoothed out the rumples in Buddy's sleeping bag and surveyed his work. The pillows looked unusually plump. He felt beneath them, then slid his hand inside the bottom one's case. Beyond the scrunched-up pillow was his backpack.

Cam bit his lip, his heart pounding in his chest. He checked outside once more, saw no one. Quick! Look inside! Guilt stayed his hand. But it was *his* backpack. And his flute. If anyone caught him, he'd have nothing to apologize for. With new resolve, he pulled out the pillow, unzipped the backpack, and peered inside.

There was his flute case, and his music pouch. And beside them lay the can of lighter fluid. Cam's pulse quickened. All he had to do was grab the instrument and go give it to Pee Wee, ask him to put it away for safe-keeping. He wouldn't even have to rat on Buddy and the whole crazy spy-thing would be over. As he pulled the case from the book bag, he winced at the sharp fumes now rising from it.

Had the lighter fluid spilled on his flute? No, the cap was jammed, remember? Maybe while he was giving stuff to Pee Wee, he ought to get rid of the lighter fluid, too. At the rate Buddy and Jason were escalating this stupid game, Cam would be a fool to let either one of them have it. Who knew *what* they'd do next?

Pulling out his towel, he wrapped up the flute case and the can and tried to look casual, the awkward bundle tucked beneath one arm. All at once, the enormity of what he was about to do hit him full force. Even if he never said a word to Pee Wee, none of the guys would believe he hadn't ratted on them. Besides, they were so intent on stealing one anothers' spoils and being named camp generals that Cam's surrendering a sure winner like the lighter fluid was bound to make them all see red. They'd brand him a traitor, write him off, refuse to speak to him. Cam might as well spend the next seven weeks in solitary confinement.

He swallowed hard as he pronounced his own sentence. Being here for the summer was bad enough, he thought. But if all four tentmates rejected him, it'd be absolutely unbearable.

Then an alternate plan popped into this mind. What if he gave Pee Wee only his flute and hid the lighter fluid himself? At least that way he could be sure that everyone would be safe. Each team would think the other had stolen it. And best of all, Pee Wee wouldn't be coming down on them for keeping the can in the first place. The plan was brilliant, if he *did* say so himself.

Biting his lip, Cam considered what to do first. If he went to find Pee Wee, someone might be here when he got back. On the other hand, if he hid the lighter fluid first, he could always saunter off with his flute-bundle and no one would be the wiser.

Grabbing the can, he set down his wrapped-up case and scanned the tent for an unlikely hiding place. His suitcase and bunk were out of the question, the first places Buddy would look. The rafters? Too obvious. What about under the floor? He dropped to his knees to examine the possibility, crawling the length of the planks in search of access. There it was—beneath the back steps!

He cracked the door, leaned out, and slid the can under the tent. But it was still visible between the wooden slats. Cam sighed. He'd come too far to give up now. A delivery truck bounced past on the service road, churning up dust. He ducked behind the door to avoid breathing it in. Of course! That was it!

His heartbeat thrummed in his ears as he eyed the towel bundle on his bunk. What if Buddy came in? Surely he'd see it sitting there, see the backpack laid open on the bed too, and *then* what would he do? Grab the flute and head straight for the lake to make good his threat? Maybe it'd be safer, Cam decided, to store the instrument in his backpack. Inside Buddy's pillowcase.

Just for a few minutes. Just in case. And if the worst happened, well, Mick *had* promised to take care of it, hadn't he?

Cam swallowed hard as he returned the instrument to its former hiding place. Would he have enough time to go back for it? He didn't know. But it was a gamble he had to take. Cam figured if he had to, he could live without his flute for a few more days. But with a lighter-fluid accident on his conscience? No way. He felt badly enough about what had happened to Joey with the trap.

Creeping outside, he flattened himself beside the steps and began scooping handfuls of fine brown dust over the rectangular can. At last it was indistinguishable from its surroundings. Pleased with the effort, Cam brushed himself off and went back inside. No sooner had the back door thumped shut than the front door squeaked open.

Struggling to swallow his surprise at seeing Buddy, Cam eyed the spot on his bunk where only minutes earlier his bundle had lain. If only he could have hurried a bit faster, he might have been able to rescue his flute. But as Dad always said: "Close only counts in horseshoes." Now, as he tried to force the disappointment from his face, he could finally understand at gut level the wisdom in that little saying. His stomach knotted with resignation. All he could do now was count on Mick to keep his word.

"What's taking you, gook?"

Cam balled and unballed his fists at his sides. The familiar heat rushed to his cheeks. There had to be something—some name, some sore spot—that would get to Buddy in a way that no well-placed punch ever could. Narrowing his gaze, Cam glared up at Buddy, wondering what it might be, and did not reply.

"Fine. *Don't* answer. What do I care?" Buddy said. "Just tell me, what'd you do with Mick?"

"Mick?" Cam could only blink. Surely Buddy hadn't overheard their conversation about the flute. But did he seem suspicious? At last Cam found words and willed them to sound light. "Oh, he's got poison ivy, didn't you know? He's up at the nurse's."

Buddy grunted. "That doesn't explain what you're doing here, all by yourself."

"Me?" Cam stole a glance at Buddy's neatly made bed and wondered whether Buddy'd notice the improvement. He hoped not. It'd be a sure tip-off that he'd been snooping around. "I—I was just reading a letter from home." Cam nodded toward the pink envelope on his bunk.

"S'pose you just can't *wait* for Visitors Day, right?" Buddy said. When Cam nodded, he laughed bitterly. "Well, stick around, gook. It ought to be a real riot."

EIGHT

SUNDAY MORNING CAM sat cross-legged on the ridge overlooking the parking lot. Mick's grandparents had arrived from their home in Milwaukee right after breakfast, and Whaler's whole family had just piled out of a van, bearing grocery sacks overflowing with popcorn, chips, and cookies. With a sigh, Cam hugged his knees to his chest and scanned the arriving cars.

"No show, huh?" Jason flopped down beside him. "Mine aren't coming either. They're off at one of my old lady's art fairs. Could be anywhere."

"Mine'll be here," Cam said. "It's still early."

"Yeah, well." Jason tossed a pine needle at Cam. "You can hang out with me if they don't make it."

Cam scowled, said nothing. Of course they'd make it. Why wouldn't they?

"How's Operation Buddy going? What did you find out?"

Cam hesitated. Should he tell Jason that he'd taken the lighter fluid and hidden it under Olympus? That would show Cam's loyalty, all right. But somehow he felt safer with the flammable liquid out of everyone's hands. If only there were a way to prove himself and turn this whole spy business to his advantage at the same time . . .

"Well?" Jason said.

"Matter of fact"—Cam looked around and lowered his voice to a whisper—"I think I know where they're hiding their spoils."

Jason's eyes widened. "You do?"

"Uh-huh. Try looking in a gray backpack. Inside one of Buddy's pillowcases."

"Really?"

Cam nodded, explaining that he'd discovered it before breakfast while plumping Buddy's pillows. The half-truth made his heart race. Actually, he'd only been reassuring himself that Buddy hadn't moved the pack since Cam's discovery on Tuesday. But Jason didn't need to know that, did he?

"Buddy didn't see you?"

"Nah," Cam said. "He was down at the bathroom." Thank goodness Mountain Man hadn't made them play another round of the game. The few days' break had obviously made Buddy and Mick cocky; they hadn't even bothered to check on their spoils. The fools.

"Can you believe that?" Jason said. "It's been right

under our noses." He shook his head. "What say we go steal it?"

"Right now? There's people all over the place."

"Exactamundo!" Jason tipped his black fedora in salute to his genius. "And no one'll be paying any attention to us."

"I don't know." Buddy seemed to have a sixth sense; hadn't he just missed catching Cam red-handed with the lighter fluid the other day? And hadn't Buddy foiled Cam's attempt to steal back his flute? What if he caught Cam today? Would he really deep-six the instrument in the lake? "Why don't *you* get it?" Cam said at last. "You're better at these things than I am."

"You think so? All right!" Jason slapped Cam five and preened as he stood up. "Well," he said, "you gonna sit here all day or what?"

Cam shrugged. Only till they get here, he thought.

"Suit yourself. I'm going to go try to get that backpack, while I have a chance."

"I'll bet you anything it's still there. Good luck." Cam waved and Jason started up the trail toward main camp. More cars and an RV rolled into the parking lot, but there was no sign of his parents' gray Volvo. Several boys darted out of the trees, down the incline, and into their parents' outstretched arms. He bit his lip to keep it from quivering, and turned away, unable to watch. Where are they? Did they have an accident?

The RV chugged to a halt in a parking space just below him. A tall, gaunt man clambered out and, favoring his right leg, made his way around the vehicle. To

Cam's surprise, Buddy strode toward him, a look of disgust hardening his face.

"Where's Mom?" he demanded.

Mr. Fiedler offered an exaggerated palms-up gesture in reply.

"Answer me! Why didn't she come?"

"Work. Business. As usual."

"That figures." Buddy eyed his father critically. "You must have started real early. Look at you."

"You watch your mouth, boy. Think you're too big to get your wagon fixed?"

Cam swallowed hard, tried to make sense of their conversation, but there was something missing. What was Buddy so mad about? he wondered, inching backward toward the trees. Buddy wouldn't like him listening, would probably flatten Cam's face if he knew he'd heard. Flatten my face. Cam grunted at the irony. Yeah, right. There had to be a better place to wait for his parents.

"Would you just get in the camper?" Buddy said, a pleading edge to his voice. "Please? So we can talk?"

"Sure. Why not?"

The doors opened and slammed shut. Cam found his feet and trudged toward Olympus. They *had* to be coming, but when? Maybe his mother had said in one of her letters; he should have read them, shouldn't have assumed they were all garbage.

As Jason had predicted, the tent was deserted. Cam checked Buddy's pillow for the backpack. Gone! Jason must have pulled it off. Relief washed through him.

Now, at least his flute was in good hands. And it wouldn't be long before it would be in *his.*

Unzipping his suitcase, Cam retrieved his mother's letters. She'd written three in a week. Four pages each, front and back—except for the first one. Ridiculous. What did he care about Mrs. Tolliver's granddaughter getting a dog or whether the McCaffreys' garden was being eaten by rabbits? No wonder he hadn't read them. But now he had no choice.

Flopping on his bunk, he pulled out the first letter and tried without success to concentrate. What was the deal with Buddy and his father? Were they fighting out in the camper—or merely talking as Buddy had said? Just forget them, he thought. Get on with it. He forced himself to wade through pages of university news—how summer school was going, what her students were like—and neighborhood gossip—would you believe that they're trying to build a community pool again? and guess who's having this year's block party?—before he found what he was looking for.

"Professor Brainerd will be here this weekend for a conference," his mother had written. "Dad studied under him at Cornell, so there's no possible way we can get out of entertaining him and his wife. I hope you understand why we won't be able to make Visitors Day. I promise—cross my heart—that we'll be there next week, okay?"

No, Cam thought. It's not. He crumpled the page and rolled onto his side, blinking back tears. Jason was right; they weren't coming after all. And he had been so sure that he could have talked them into taking him home. Now he had to hold on till next week, and who knew what could happen in the meantime? It wasn't fair!

Closing his eyes, he tamped down the stuffy feeling in his throat. He didn't belong here. The whole situation was impossible. First Buddy and his name-calling. Then the stupid war game and Buddy's making off with Cam's flute. And now Cam's role as a double agent, walking a tightrope between his friends and his enemies. How could Mom and Dad abandon him at a time like this?

If only there were a way to escape. Sleep. Maybe sleep would do the trick. Cam rubbed his forehead, easing the tension away as his mother often did when he had a headache. Gradually he worked his breathing into a relaxing pattern—in-two-three, out-two-three, slow and even. He'd dream happy thoughts, something light. Like his flute concerto echoing through the rec room, fingers flying, notes soaring, singing in his soul.

Voices. Outside. Strained and hushed. Footfalls on the wooden steps—*thu-thunk, thu-thunk.* Cam blinked away his dream, reoriented himself in the tent.

"Yeah?" came a man's voice. "And I don't guess that was a little gook I seen runnin' around here last week either, was it?"

Gook! They're talking about me. Cam burrowed beneath his sleeping bag, pressing himself into the shadow of Jason's bunk. His heartbeat mimicked the footsteps outside. As the door scraped open, he held his breath.

"He's no gook." Buddy sighed. "He's Korean."

"Ha!" Aluminum crackled and clunked to the floor. "Gook, Korean. Whatsa difference? Both too yellow to fight their own wars. Hafta drag us in to do it for 'em."

"The war's over, Dad. Let it go."

"Mine isn't."

Beneath the sleeping bag, Cam struggled against the mounting heat. His breath came back to him, warm and stale. How much longer could he hide? Papers rustled in the wastebasket, followed by the thunk of metal hitting bottom.

"And quit cleanin' up after me," Mr. Fiedler snapped.

"It's eleven A.M., for crying out loud! What if Pee Wee came in here and saw you drunk again? Last week wasn't enough?"

A sharp, cracking sound pierced the air. "Don't you talk to me like that! I'm still your father. And you're not too big to take a strap to, you hear?"

Sneaking a peek above the covers, Cam could see the red imprint of a hand on Buddy's cheek. Buddy wadded his fists, breathed through clenched teeth. "You touch me again, and I swear I'll . . . I'll . . ." He broke off with a sob.

"You'll what? You'll nothin', you little coward." Mr. Fiedler raked his fingers through his graying hair. "Been hangin' around that gook too much, that it? Maybe I oughta get your tent changed."

Buddy tossed his hair, revealing a glimpse of scar. "Been hanging around *you* too much," he muttered.

"Wha's that?"

Buddy cleared his throat. "I said maybe you just better get out of here, while you still can walk. Go sleep it off in the camper."

His father stared at Buddy's forehead for a long moment, then reached out to touch the scar. Buddy flinched, blocked his hand.

"Don't you pull away, boy. Get over here and let me look at that." Buddy held his ground. "I'm talkin' to you," Mr. Fiedler said. "I wanna see how it's healin'."

"Like you really care, right?" Buddy's visible eye flashed. "You just don't want there to be any evidence."

"What do I know about evidence? That's your mama-the-big-deal-lawyer-lady's thing, not mine."

"Yeah," Buddy said. "And you can't stand that, can you?" He paced to the door, pulled it open for his father, his eyes downcast. "Will you just go now? Or are you gonna wait for Pee Wee to take you, like last time?"

Mr. Fiedler blew out a long breath. "Okay. I'm goin'." As he passed Buddy, he tipped Buddy's chin upward. "You still wearin' my dog tags?" Buddy nodded. A trace of smile softened Mr. Fiedler's profile. "Believe me, son. I made it out of *that* war," he said, "and I'm gonna make it out of this'n. You'll see. I'll get myself a new shrink. Go back to AA. It's gonna be different this time. I promise."

"Yeah. Right."

Mr. Fiedler shook his head sadly. "This here's one battle I sure wish you coulda missed."

"Me too, Dad," Buddy said. "Me too."

Mr. Fiedler squeezed Buddy's shoulder, cleared his throat. "I . . . I really do . . . love you, son."

Buddy blinked quickly and touched the corner of his eye. He bit his lip and nodded. "Go on, Dad," he whispered. "Just get out of here."

Cam's heart raced as he ducked back under the sleeping bag. Mr. Fiedler thumped down the stairs, his gait uneven. At last the door banged shut, and Buddy shuffled toward his bunk. The springs groaned as he lay down.

Cam wondered if he dared reveal his presence. He'd tell Buddy that now he understood. It was his father's war; it didn't have to be Buddy's as well. Cam rehearsed what he'd say, how he'd say it. But fear froze the words to his tongue. Maybe he, Cam, *was* a coward after all, just like Mr. Fiedler had said. But it had nothing to do with his being Korean, or adopted, or even American—and everything to do with his just being human.

A grating sound drifted over from Buddy's bunk—his father's dog tags, scraping against the chain. Not tough and threatening this time, but rather wistful. "The war's over, Dad," Buddy muttered. "And everybody lost." There was an eerie silence, followed by the *thunk-swish* of metal hitting the floor.

Cam swallowed hard, and let the gesture speak for them both. Outside something bumped up against the tent, shattering the moment. Laughter drifted off the knoll, turned into a party of voices.

"I'll get it!" a child cried.

"No, let me. I wanna. It's my ball."

Buddy's bunk creaked, but Cam dared not look to see what he was doing. Mumbling something, Buddy pummeled his pillows. "Hey," he said, surprised. Then, *"Hey!"*

The backpack! How could Cam have forgotten? His heart hammered in his ears. He fought for breath. Be invisible. Disappear. If only he could! Buddy was sure to discover him now.

Footsteps tripped up the steps, into the tent. "Mommy, look!" came a little girl's voice. "Jonah put my picture up."

Shoes screeched across the floor. "I promised, didn't I?" Whaler said.

The child giggled as if she were being tickled, and Cam allowed himself a momentary pang of envy. For years he'd wanted a brother or sister, had almost had one once, but for Mom's miscarriage. Was he himself enough for his parents? Or did he need his talent to make up for being their only child—and an adopted one at that?

"Aren't you going to introduce us to your friend?" a woman asked.

"My friend?" Whaler said. "Oh, yeah." He lowered his voice. "I didn't see him. Looks like he's taking a nap or something. Maybe we ought to clear out."

"Oh. I'm sorry, I meant . . ." The woman's voice trailed off.

"Him?" Whaler scoffed. "That's Buddy."

Cam feigned sleep, his heart beating a cadence of thank you, thank you, thank you. Whaler was an absolute genius. For all Buddy knew, Cam *had* been napping. And hadn't heard a thing.

Buddy mumbled a greeting to Mrs. Wainwright, then cleared his throat. "Whaler . . . uh . . . I don't suppose you know anything about a missing backpack, do you?"

"What color?"

"Gray."

"What's in it?"

"As if you didn't know," Buddy said. "Never mind. I'll find it myself." He stomped out of the cabin. The door slammed behind him.

Sweaty and relieved, Cam chuckled to himself as he peeled back the covers. Whaler was the only one who *didn't* know about the backpack, yet Buddy was still suspicious. For the first time, Cam could understand why. He guessed that when a kid had a father like Buddy's, trust wasn't exactly second nature.

"Hey, sorry we woke you," Whaler said. "Your folks didn't show?" Cam shook his head glumly. "Too bad. What's eating Fiedler anyway?"

"Oh, the usual." Cam shrugged, not wanting to explain further. Whaler was bound to find out anyway—about the flute *and* the stolen spoils. It was just a matter of time. But there was no sense spilling the whole thing in front of the Wainwrights. Let Whaler enjoy their visit, he thought. It'll be war as usual as soon as they're gone.

NINE

DINNER CLEANUP WAS Olympus's reward at the end of Visitors Day. Pee Wee outlined the various chores—scraping plates, busing dishes, sweeping, and helping out in the kitchen—and before anyone else could volunteer, Mick and Buddy headed off toward the dish room. Cam had snatched a broom and started for the farthest corner of the mess hall, when someone grabbed his arm. Hard.

He whirled about, somehow expecting to see Buddy. But it was Jason who faced him down. "What's the big idea?" Cam said, shaking off Jason's hold.

"That's what I should be asking you."

"I—I don't know what you mean."

"Just whose side are you on anyway?" Jason asked.

"Ours . . . yours. I told you before."

"Yeah? Well, there was nothing *in* that backpack."

"Nothing?" Cam's voice squeaked. What about his flute?

"Least ways, not our lighter fluid."

Good, Cam thought. My flute *is* there.

"I *know* they took it," Jason continued. "I saw them with my own two eyes." He nailed Cam with an accusing stare. "I don't suppose you have any idea where it went, right?"

Cam moved his head slowly from side to side, did his best to look Jason in the eye. He wondered if telling the truth would be any easier.

"You mean you never saw it?"

"No," Cam said. "They must have hidden it someplace. How should I know where?"

Jason did not reply. He tipped his head as if sizing Cam up.

"Jeez, Jase. What kind of a friend do you think I am?" Cam swallowed the answer to his own question. "You think I'd help *them?*"

"No. Of course not," Jason said, his face relaxing into a smile. "I was just kidding, okay?"

"Well, I should hope so." Cam feigned indignation, punched Jason's arm in jest. Did Jason trust him again? He just *had* to. Then Cam could ask about his flute and be certain that he'd get it back. For the moment, at least, it was out of Buddy's hands. That was the main thing. In the meantime, Cam would just have to prove that he really *was* on Jason's side, no matter how things looked.

"Tell you what," Jason said. "I've got something of

Buddy's. Something he'd do *anything* to get back." He grinned mysteriously.

"What is it?"

Before Jason could reply, Pee Wee called, "Hey, you two!" from where he and Whaler were scraping slop off the plates and into the garbage. "Get to work, will you? Jason, we need you to bus."

Jason pulled out a bench, making no move to leave, and Cam started sweeping under the table. "What've you got?" he whispered. "What do you want me to do?"

Footsteps echoed through the great room as Pee Wee strode toward them. "Lowman," he said, "quit kissing off and give us a hand with these dishes. We're going to be here all night at this rate. And you know what that means."

"What?"

"No night games down at the lake."

Jason shrugged. "Those aren't so great. At least last year we had fireworks."

"Aw, come on. It'll be fun. I'm in charge of the greased watermelon relay."

"All right, all right. What can I say? You got me." Jason turned to Cam. "I'll tell you later. Stand by."

"Roger," Cam said. "Over and out."

Jason nodded a couple times, but Cam had the feeling it was not at him. The unfocused glee in Jason's eyes suggested that something else was going on beneath that black fedora. As Cam watched him go, a rash of goose bumps skittered down his arms.

What was he up to anyway? The question haunted

Cam the length and width of the mess hall and up until the time they were changing into their swimsuits for the evening's lakeside activities. Jason was the first to sling his towel over his shoulder and head out. Buddy followed close behind.

"What's their hurry?" Pee Wee asked.

"Search me," Whaler said. "But I wouldn't leave 'em alone too long, if I were you." He cinched up his trunks and tried to push his stomach into hiding. "Why'd they have to bring me all that junk?" He groaned, eyeing the empty food wrappers on his bunk.

Mick climbed up on his and hung his head over the edge. "Question is, why'd *you* have to eat it?"

"Now, now," Pee Wee said. "Let's be kind, okay?"

Mick grumbled something and Whaler wadded the wrappers, throwing them away. Cam dropped to his hands and knees in search of his rubber thongs.

"How's your poison ivy?" Pee Wee asked. "You up for some games?"

Mick shook his head. "Nah. Better not."

"Too bad. Not even to watch? It'll be fun. Cam, you coming?"

"In a minute," he said. "You go on. I'll catch up."

Pee Wee pulled back the mosquito netting and rolled two watermelons off his bed. "Whaler, here. Give me a hand."

Whaler tucked one under each arm as if they were footballs. Pee Wee managed the other two, and Cam opened the door. "See you down there, okay?" Pee Wee said.

Cam nodded and let the door clap shut behind them. Spying his thongs beneath Buddy's bunk, he reached under to get them. Mick clicked on his boombox. Strains of classical guitar wove through the tent as he flopped on his back and stared up at the ceiling.

Cam's jaw sagged open in surprise as he scrambled to his feet. "Is that tape yours?"

"Yep."

"Thought you were into heavy metal."

"So?" Mick rolled onto his side, propping his head with his hand. "What if I am?"

Cam shrugged. "Nothing. I just didn't expect you to have . . . well, maybe you're different than you seem."

"Aren't we all."

Cam pressed his lips together, eyed the floor, knew Mick was talking about his flute. "Yeah," he said at last. "I guess so."

"I wish they'd let me bring my guitar. Too big, they said. Something will happen to it."

Cam grunted. "They're right. Be glad you didn't."

"Don't sweat it," Mick said. "The game's almost over. Only one more session, from what I hear. You'll get it back soon."

"Yeah." Cam tried to muster some conviction, reminded himself that Jason had his flute now. "I'm sure I will." He forced a smile and grabbed his towel. "You coming? Just to watch?"

Mick shook his head. "Wouldn't want to get thrown in."

"Who'd do a thing like that?"

"Jason. Buddy, maybe. Just to be funny."

"I don't get it." Cam sighed. "What are you afraid of? The water's waist deep."

Mick sat up and dangled his legs. He scratched at a spaghetti stain in the middle of his shirt placket. "Aagh! Where's that spot remover?" He slid to the floor and rummaged through his suitcase, locating a small vial at last. "This better work or my mom'll kill me."

"Mick, come on. I'm not going to tell anyone."

"It's no big deal," Mick said, still scrubbing at the stain.

Cam blew out a long breath, but said nothing.

"Look, I almost drowned once. That's it. All right? Case closed."

"Oh, Mick." A wave of sympathy knocked him off-balance. "I . . . I didn't know."

"Like I said, it's no big deal."

Yes, it is, Cam thought. And you told me, of all people. Sharing Mick's secret warmed him like hot cocoa on a wintry day. "Well, see you. Look," he said, "why don't I just tell Pee Wee you've got a stomachache or something?"

"Thanks but . . ." Mick glanced up from his shirt. "Sure," he said. "Why not?"

Cam nudged open the door. "Catch you later, okay?"

"Yeah. Later."

Grinning at the classical guitar music he left behind in his wake, Cam headed off toward the waterfront. Who would have thought that he and Mick might have something in common? As he passed the lodge, Whaler hustled out of the rest room entrance. "Psst! Cam!" He motioned him over.

"What's going on?"

"It's Jason. I don't know what he's up to, man, but it's—I don't know—big."

Cam frowned. "Big?"

"Look. I'm supposed to tell you to get Buddy and Mick over to the Swamp. During the watermelon relay."

"What for?"

Whaler shrugged. "He won't tell me. But he says we won't be disappointed."

"I don't know." What could Jason be planning? Nothing dangerous, that was for sure. Cam had the lighter fluid. Besides, he had to prove his loyalty so he could reclaim his flute. . . .

"He says this'll clinch the game. Buddy'll back off and we'll win. No sweat. Come on, Cam," Whaler said. "Whose side are you on, anyway?"

There were those words again: Whose side are you on? He hardly knew anymore. The lines were blurring in his mind. He looked up at Whaler, read the urgency in his eyes. "Okay, okay," he said wearily. "I'll do it. Tell Jason he can count on me."

The night games were just starting as Cam wove his way through the other campers toward Buddy. The taller boy was fondling a ripe water balloon and positioned it over Cam's head when he drew close. "Think I should?" he said.

"Suit yourself. But I've gotta talk to you and Mick. Like, right away."

Buddy massaged the balloon but did not make it burst. "So?"

"Not here," Cam said. "Up at Olympus."

Buddy yawned, pretending boredom. "Later. Can't you see I'm busy?"

Cam sighed, racked his brain for an angle, some way to convince Buddy to go with him. Now. And then it came to him—the sore spot that'd knock Buddy off-balance. "You want everyone to know how you got that scar?" he said, lowering his voice.

Buddy narrowed his gaze. "What'd you say?"

"You heard me," Cam said, his heart pumping him full of false courage. "I know. All about your dad and . . . and everything."

"How could you?" Buddy's hand flew to his forehead.

"I wasn't asleep, that's how," Cam said. "I heard the whole thing."

"You little creep. Say one word and—"

"I'm not kidding around, Buddy." Cam nailed him with the most intimidating glare he could muster. *Jason* had his flute now, not Buddy. Cam could afford to be brazen. Just like Tom Phan. Well, almost. "You coming or do I talk?"

Buddy managed a reluctant nod and nudged Cam forward. As Cam pressed through the crowd, he noticed Jason standing off to one side. Edging past, Cam gave him a thumbs-up sign.

"Hey, Lowman," Buddy called. "Think fast."

Jason's head jerked upward as Buddy's balloon arced toward him and splattered at his feet. Cam cringed, expecting to be caught in the middle of a retaliatory strike. Instead, Jason just stood there, grinning, pouring his own balloon from one hand to the other.

"What's wrong with *him?*" Buddy asked.

"I don't know. That's what I've got to talk to you and Mick about." Cam chose the service road route to the cabin, slipping among the long dusky shadows rather than risking exposure on the more barren hill. He was getting good at this, turning into a regular little spy. Fun. Wasn't that what he was having?

"You're just bluffing," Buddy said. "About my father, I mean."

Cam stared him down. "What do you think?"

Buddy tossed his head, said nothing. By the time they got to the tent, he was champing with anxiety. "You wouldn't say anything, right? He doesn't mean it. It's the booze gets him going." Buddy grabbed Cam's arm as he reached for the door. "Come on, man. They could lock him up, take him away."

"Would that really be so bad?" Cam said.

"He's my *father.*"

"Yeah, right." Cam avoided the desperation in Buddy's eye. "He sure doesn't act like one."

"Please . . . Cam." He loosened his grasp on Cam's arm.

Amazing! Cam blinked at the sound of his name on Buddy's tongue, and felt suddenly, crazily, as if he'd just grown six inches. "Oh, you know me," he said sarcastically. "I'm real good at keeping secrets."

Buddy released Cam's arm, and, with an embarrassed

shrug, followed him into the tent. Mick abruptly clicked off his guitar tape and snapped in some heavy metal. "Hey," he said, color rising in his cheeks. "What brings you two up here?"

"Jason's getting suspicious," Cam said. "I've got to prove I'm on his side by getting you guys to go to the Swamp."

"Why can't this dumb game be over already?" Mick said. "It's getting old fast."

"I know. I think so, too. But will you do it?"

Mick sighed. "Fiedler, just give him back his flute so we can stop all this monkeying around, okay?"

Buddy twisted his lips to one side and eyed the floor. "I—I don't have it."

"Jason does," Cam added.

"*Lowman* does?" Buddy said. "I should have known."

Mick cursed. "How'd you let *that* happen? God, Buddy." He glared up at his screaming boombox and punched the button for silence. "Just tell us what we're supposed to do."

Cam repeated Jason's request.

Buddy paced the floor. "What's that little weasel up to? You know, don't you?"

Cam shook his head, and Buddy scowled.

"Even if he *did* know," Mick said, "why should he tell us? Do you blame him? God, I'd kill if someone touched my guitar."

"I'm sure it's nothing dangerous," Cam said. "Probably a trick. Something we'll all laugh about in a couple of days. Like maybe a water balloon ambush or something."

Buddy seemed unconvinced. Mick glanced at his watch. "We'd better go," he said, leaping off his bunk. He pulled a beach towel out of his suitcase.

"What's that for?" Cam asked.

"Appearances." Mick winked. "If anyone asks, we took a detour on the way to the lake."

As they slipped out the back door, Cam glanced beneath the steps to where he'd buried the lighter fluid. Shadows bathed the area and he couldn't see whether or not the dirt had been disturbed. But why would it be? He'd done a great job in hiding it. Still, he couldn't shake off a vague feeling of dread. Maybe it had something to do with that strange grin on Jason's face during dinner cleanup. "Why don't you guys go on?" he said. "I'll be there in a minute."

"Sure you will." Buddy hiked up one corner of his mouth.

"I will. I promise."

Mick's Adam's apple bobbed. "Trust him, Buddy." He looked Cam squarely in the face.

"Believe me," Cam said, wondering why anyone should. "I'll be right there."

TEN

CAM WATCHED BUDDY and Mick shrink behind the ridge, their heads finally disappearing from view. Then he flattened himself in the dirt, reached beneath the step with a stick, and scraped at the burial spot. Metal caught the fading light, clinked upon impact with the twig. His breath rushed out in a grateful *whoosh.*

Within seconds he had exhumed the can of lighter fluid and sat spraddle-legged in the dust, placing the can between his knees. It felt the same as when he'd buried it—half-full. Yet something nagged at him. Something he couldn't quite explain. Half-full. Hadn't it seemed emptier when they'd found it? Cam frowned. Was he imagining things? He picked up the can and shook it. Definitely fuller. But that was impossible unless . . .

He grasped the cap, bracing himself for a struggle, but the top turned effortlessly. Hadn't it been stuck before? Yes, he was sure it had been. That's why they hadn't emptied it. His pulse quickened. He chewed the inside of his cheek. What was going on here? Uneasiness kneaded his stomach. He sniffed the contents. Dumb. Of course it would smell like lighter fluid. He poured some in his hand and smelled . . . nothing strong. Just a faint whiff, left over from the can.

It was water, not lighter fluid! It had to be. Cam's mind raced to make sense of it, and settled on only one explanation: Jason. He must have substituted the water back at the archery shed when he sent Cam to spy on Buddy and Mick. But why? And what had he done with the lighter fluid?

The wine bottle. Of course! Cam jumped to his feet, upsetting the can. Water cut a dark swath through the dust. Something big. That's what Whaler had said. "Oh, my God!" What could be bigger than homemade fireworks?

He tore downhill, the towel he'd draped about his neck flapping like broken wings. "Buddy! Mick!" he yelled across the playing field.

Mick turned, waved in reply.

Cam's rubber thongs slapped his heels, slowed his pace. His heart was in his throat as he hollered their names once more. At last, panting, he reached the edge of the Swamp, near where Joey had been caught in the trap.

"You guys . . . sorry . . . didn't know . . . Jason

has . . . lighter fluid." He bent over, braced his hands on his knees, struggling for breath. "Gotta get . . . out of . . . here."

"What's this?" Buddy said. "Another game? Of course he has it. That's news?"

Cam shook his head. "Listen to me. I mean it. I think Jason's making—I don't know—a bomb or something."

"Get real." Buddy tossed his hair.

"Maybe we should listen to him," Mick said.

"Are you kidding? He's got no reason to spy for us anymore. It's a trick I tell you. A setup."

The sun hovered low over the lake, bathing the field in long, red-edged shadows. Cam scanned the clearing, his breath coming easier now. At least there was no sign of Jason or Whaler. Maybe the only thing on my side is time, he thought. *My* side. Whatever that means. He sighed and stared at the ground as Buddy and Mick argued in hushed tones.

A chameleon, dusty brown, darted through the sunburned grass, narrowly missing his toes. Cam watched it scurry a couple of feet to the edge of the Swamp, where it gradually greened up and disappeared amid its surroundings. Goose bumps tripped down his arms, across his bare chest. That's me, he thought. The original Mr. Camouflage. Always trying to blend in. And disappear. He shook his head, swallowed hard. "You guys! Shut up!"

Both heads flipped in his direction.

Cam's throat went dry. His pulse quickened. "There's something I've . . . got to tell you. About the game. About . . . me." Cam looked from Mick to Buddy, wet his lips, and pressed on. "You made me spy on my team and—

"So?" Buddy said. "What else is new?"

Cam struggled to find his voice again. "I . . . I was spying on you, too."

"What the—" Buddy curled a fist and raised it to Cam's face, but Mick stepped between them.

"Leave him alone, man. Hear him out."

"I don't know what else to say except . . . I'm sorry. I didn't want to play the stupid game in the first place. I—I just wanted to fit in."

"Well, you've got a great way of doing it, gook."

Mick's eyes flashed. "Say that word again, Buddy, and I'll make you eat it."

Cam grinned despite his best efforts. That goes double for me, he thought. Buddy hung his head. At last he glared at Cam. "So what's this all about, huh? First you drag us down here. Now you want us to leave."

"It's Jason, don't you see? He must have guessed I was spying for you." Cam was pacing back and forth now, thoughts coming fast. "Sure! That's it! That's why he poured out the lighter fluid. And all along I thought we were safe. Nothing bad could happen. Because *I* had it, only I didn't."

"You lost me," Mick said.

"Never mind, never mind. We don't have time for that now. We've got to stop him, don't you see?"

"Jason's weird but he's no mad bomber," Buddy said. "Get real."

"This is as real as it gets." Cam sighed. He was getting nowhere with Buddy. But maybe Mick would help. And if not, well, he guessed he'd have to handle it himself. "All right, *don't* believe me. Do what you want. But I'm gonna go stop him before it's too late." Cam stalked off across the playing field.

"Hey, wait up!" Mick called, jogging after him.

"Yoo-hoo! Oh, gir-ls!" a phony, high-pitched voice floated down from higher ground, tinged with an echo. "You're for-get-ting some-thing."

Cam and Mick locked stares before turning toward the voice. A daub of black stained the ridge overlooking the Swamp.

"You girls lose something?" Jason's laughter tumbled after his words.

A twig snapped. Cam flinched, spun about, collided with Mick. "Whaler, jeez!" Cam struggled for composure. "What are *you* doing here?"

"Playing lookout."

"Lookout?" Mick said, his tone thick with scorn.

Whaler shrugged. "Just following orders. Same as you."

Cam grunted. Whaler had *that* right.

"Yoo-hoo, Bud-dy! Say good-bye to your spoi-ls," Jason sang out.

"What's he talking about?" Mick said.

"Buddy's backpack. Look!" Whaler pointed toward the old dead tree in the Swamp. There, lashed among the branches, was the gray backpack.

"That's not Buddy's. That's mine." Cam willed his

legs to move but they were cemented to the spot.

"Man, your flute's in there!" Mick said. He was jogging in place, his back toward the tree. "You hear me? Your flute!" When Cam didn't budge, Mick turned and charged across the field, shouting at Buddy, who was heading off toward the lake. But Buddy just shook his head and kept walking.

Something flashed on the ridge. From this distance, Cam couldn't be sure. But it looked like fire. No! Jason wouldn't, would he? Kicking off his rubber thongs in order to run faster, Cam sprinted toward the overlook. Whaler called after him, but Cam didn't answer. Prickers nipped his bare feet and an occasional stone hobbled his stride but he pressed on, his lungs bursting. Halfway up the path to the ridge he caught sight of Mick, climbing the tree.

"Mick!" He waved wildly. "Get out of there!"

But Mick either did not see or hear, or chose not to listen. Cam cursed and pumped his legs faster. Coming up the rise, he spotted Jason hovering over the wine bottle, lighting something that flopped out of its mouth.

"Jason! Don't!" Too late. The wick had caught flame and was spitting like a sparkler.

Starting at Cam's voice, Jason grabbed the bottle and edged closer to the rocky drop-off. "You little traitor," he said. "Think I'm stupid? I knew all along what you were up to. And I thought we were friends."

Cam held his distance, but gathered two handfuls of dirt. He could see Mick still struggling to free the backpack from the tree, and swallowed hard. "Be mad at me.

I deserve it. I *was* spying on you. But I had my reasons. Come on, Jason. Listen to me. Put that out. We'll talk."

"No way."

"Don't do this. Someone's gonna get hurt."

Jason laughed. "That's what *you* think. I've got it covered. Now get out of my way." He shoved Cam aside, cocking his arm.

Mick! Get out of the Swamp! Cam's mind screamed as he lunged forward, flinging dirt at the bottle, at Jason. He didn't know which. Didn't care. Jason grunted, collapsing beneath him, and in the same moment, a shattering *whoosh* exploded on the rocks.

Cam scrambled to his feet, untangling himself from his towel. Jason shoved him from behind. "Now look what you've done!" he yelled.

Parched weeds crackled up in flame along the rocky ledge. Jason grabbed his towel, flailed it at the fire. "Don't just stand there, Cam! Help me!"

"They need to be wet!" Cam said. "Down at the shed! Hurry!"

He bolted for the path as Whaler puffed his way to the top. "He's gone crazy, man," Whaler said. "What're we gonna do?"

"Water! Quick! Follow me!"

With Cam in the lead, the two boys charged down the trail, angling left toward the archery range.

"Mick," Cam panted, as he soaked his towel in the bubbler. "He okay?"

Whaler nodded. "Went to get Buddy."

"Did he get the backpack?"

"I don't think so." Whaler's legs twitched impatiently as he awaited his turn at the water. "Hurry up!"

Seconds ticked by like hours. Cam pushed away images of his flute being engulfed in flames, turning into ashes in the Swamp. All that mattered now was helping Jason put out the fire. At last he heaved the towel up and slopped it over his shoulder. "Meet you up there," he said, turning to go. "Here come Mick and Buddy."

The tall Californian jogged behind Buddy, and kept prodding him forward. "Shut up and get going," Mick said. "You're in this too."

Buddy grumbled some reply as Cam rushed past them, heading uphill. "Go wet your towels," Cam called. "I think we can put it out."

Snapping and crackling greeted him as he crested the ridge. Flames danced along the ledge and multiplied despite Jason's beating. He'd lost his fedora, and his cheeks were smudged and tear stained. As Cam rushed toward him, he cried out in relief. "I thought you'd left me."

Cam shook his head. "Come on." Heat rolled at him in waves as he waded forward, flinging his towel out ahead. A spark seared his bare foot. He yowled, hopped around on the other.

"You okay?" Jason abandoned his efforts and hurried toward him.

Cam waved him away. "Fine. Get back there."

Again and again Cam hurled his towel at the flames. Just as they seemed beaten down, they'd erupt somewhere else, prompting a new flurry of activity. At last

Whaler joined the effort. Jason seemed energized by his presence.

"We can do this, guys," Jason said. "See? It's not spreading."

Cam wasn't so sure, but he said nothing. Maybe when Mick and Buddy got here, they *could* beat it out. And no one would have to know. But none of them was dressed for this, and Cam, barefooted, least of all.

By the time Mick and Buddy arrived, the fire was creeping toward the path. "It's following the weeds around the rocks!" Mick yelled. "If it hits the Swamp, the whole camp will go!"

"No way," Jason said. "It's wet down there. Won't burn. You think I'm stupid or something? I thought of that. If Cam hadn't spoiled my aim—"

"Mick might not be standing here, helping out," Cam shot back.

Mick nodded his gratitude and started toward the ledge. "I don't care what you say, Lowman. Think you're so smart. That swamp's gonna burn for sure."

"Yeah," Buddy chimed in, "and you're gonna be in trouble up to your eyeballs, Jase. I can hardly wait."

"Stop it! All of you!" Fire danced in Whaler's eyes. "We've got to work together."

"Yeah," Jason said. "Come on. Truce. No sides anymore. We can stop this thing before anyone finds out." Buddy nodded grudgingly, Whaler and Mick, with more enthusiasm. Jason's gaze settled on Cam. "Well?" he said. *"Et tu, Brutè?"*

Brutè? Who was he? Jason had been talking about

sides. Maybe Brutè was a famous traitor or something. How should Cam know? He didn't go to some fancy school for whiz kids. Anger flared up within him. Maybe he *had* betrayed them by playing both sides against the middle. But more than that, he'd betrayed himself. He'd been so busy being who he thought they wanted him to be that none of them even knew the *real* Cam Whitney. And whose fault was that? His. How dumb to worry about being liked, he realized, when he wasn't willing to risk showing them who he really was or telling them what he really thought.

Cam hugged himself and returned Jason's stare. He had to start showing his true colors no matter what the other guys might think. No more pretending, no more taking anyone's side but his own. "No way," he said, his voice quavering just a little. "I—I think we should go get help."

"Well, think again," Jason said.

"Come on, Cam." Mick stopped beating the flames for an instant, and let his eyes do the begging.

"Yeah," Whaler chimed in. "We can put it out ourselves. I know it."

Cam waited for Buddy to try to dissuade him, but Buddy just shouldered his towel and followed Mick toward the fire line. At last he turned back and shouted, "Once a traitor, always a traitor. That how it is?"

The fire spit a spark at Cam, and it ignited near his feet. He pounded it out with his towel. But two more took root. The four of them could stay up here and fight this fire if they wanted to, Cam thought. But he had to trust his instincts; for once he had to listen to his Self. If that made him an outcast for the rest of the summer, so be it. Cam would live with his conscience. Which was more than he'd been living with so far. Somehow, he thought, Dad would want it this way: Cam might end up friendless, but at least he'd be doing what he thought was right. Tossing his towel at Jason, Cam blinked back tears that came without warning. "Maybe I'm a traitor to *you,*" he shouted at them all. "But not to me. Not anymore."

Then he spun about and did not look back as he raced downhill past the fire.

ELEVEN

MAIN CAMP COULD have been a ghost town, save for the shrieking, laughter, and occasional whistle trills that echoed up from the waterfront. Cam staggered toward the activity bell that stood like a statue in silhouette near the basketball court. Gasping for breath and trying to dislodge the stitch in his side, he grabbed the cord and heaved it with all his might. Again and again the giant clapper flailed the metal. Vibrations scuttled down Cam's arms, resounded in his head. Why wasn't anyone coming? Couldn't they hear it down at the lake?

"Fire!" he shouted. "Fire in the Swamp!"

A door slammed somewhere in the lodge. Moments later the nurse waddled out onto the deck. "What'd you say?"

Cam stopped ringing the bell. "I said fire!" He

pointed east toward the playing field. "My friends are up there! Please! You've gotta get help!"

"I'll call it in. You keep on that bell now, you hear?"

"But no one's coming," Cam said.

"They will. You just keep a-ringing."

Cam nodded and tugged the bell into action. He wished he could see more than smoky ghosts rising in the east. Mick and the others—they'd be all right, wouldn't they? Maybe he shouldn't have left them. Cam flicked away the thought. They'd made their decision, and, for once, he'd made his. Whatever happened to them up there on the ridge was no longer his responsibility.

Mountain Man and a couple of counselors rushed toward him from across the clearing. "What's wrong?" the camp director shouted.

"Fire!" Cam pointed out the location.

"Anyone up there?"

Cam nodded, gulping down his guilt. They hadn't wanted him to tell, had wanted a chance to put it out themselves. Telling made him a traitor. No, he thought. Telling might save their lives. "Mick and Buddy," he shouted back. "Jason and Whale, uh, Jonah."

Mountain Man turned to the other counselors, drawing diagrams in the air as he spoke. Then he charged off toward the playing field, while they headed back toward the lake. "Go down to the parking lot, Cam," he hollered over his shoulder. "Show the fire trucks which way."

Cam pried his fingers off the cord and raced for the

parking lot, grateful to have a mission. It didn't make up for his role in starting the fire. But at least doing something helpful distracted his conscience.

At last sirens wailed in the distance. Cam's pulse quickened as red lights flashed through the trees down by the highway. He held his ears as a fire engine and water tanker screamed into the parking lot, bounding toward him over the ruts.

Cam held his ground and pointed out the service road. "The fire's around that way. In the Swamp. Across from the ball field."

The sirens hastened the arrival of the rest of the campers and counselors. They hurried down the incline, most still wearing swimsuits and dragging towels. All eyes riveted on the trucks. One fire fighter, hanging on to the back, managed to return a few waves as the pumper sped off. Cam had no trouble finding Pee Wee in the crowd.

"Cam, you're okay! What about the others?"

Cam shrugged. "They wanted to put it out themselves. But I . . . I wasn't sure we could."

"You did the right thing, believe me." Pee Wee blew out a long breath. He shook his head. "I don't know what happened. Last I saw, you were all down at the games. And then—poof!—everybody was gone." His tan seemed to have faded since dinnertime. "I feel like—God!—it's all my fault."

"*Your* fault?" Cam blurted. "No way. You couldn't have done anything. I was the only one who could have stopped it and . . . I didn't." He hung his head, wincing as he readjusted his footing in the sharp gravel. "I was just too late."

"What are you talking about?" Pee Wee said. "What could you have stopped?"

Cam blinked up at his counselor. Whose job was it to tell? His? Jason's? All of theirs?

"Cam. Answer me."

"The war game," he said wearily. "It was getting out of hand."

Pee Wee waited expectantly, but Cam did not elaborate further. "Well," the counselor said, "maybe we should talk about this later. When the others are back."

Pee Wee sounded so sure that they *would* be. Cam wished Pee Wee's confidence would rub off on him. What if the fire cut across the path? There'd be no escape. He reassured himself that they could always head up into the kettles. But with the area like dry tinder, couldn't the fire overtake them?

"They'll be all right," Cam said, more to himself than to Pee Wee.

The counselor tousled his hair. "Course they will," he said. But his eyes avoided Cam's, focusing somewhere above and beyond him.

The wait in the parking lot seemed interminable. At last a dark station wagon jounced toward them. Pee Wee elbowed through the crowd of campers. Cam tagged after in his wake to get a better look.

The camp director, Jason, and the nurse were in the front seat, and the other three, in the back. Mountain Man rolled down the driver's window. "I've got all four of 'em," he said to Pee Wee. "But I think they'd better be checked out. Make sure everyone stays here until the fire department gives the all clear."

Pee Wee flashed a thumbs-up to the boys. But his gesture went unreturned. Before Cam could get a closer look, the car sped away into the gathering twilight. His only impression was of blackened faces and exhaustion.

"At least they're . . . okay, right?" Cam said. They were, weren't they?

"It's like I told you. They're gonna be fine." Pee Wee smiled, then glanced at his watch, the hands beginning to glow green. "Gonna be dark soon," he said.

Cam nodded and hugged himself, though he wasn't cold.

Pee Wee surveyed the restless group of campers and sighed. "Too bad you didn't grab your flute out of Olympus," he said. "I bet they'd love to hear you play."

"My flute?" Cam's voice shot up an octave. "It's in the tent?"

"Well, I . . . I don't know," Pee Wee said. "I just assumed."

"Oh." Cam's disappointment registered in the single word. It was probably still in his backpack, up in the tree. By this time, the fire could have swallowed it. There was no way to know. But at least a flute could be replaced. Unlike people. "Well," Cam said, "at least the guys are okay. That's the main thing."

Pee Wee cocked his head, regarding Cam strangely. "I think I missed something. What's your flute got to do with them being all right?"

"You wouldn't understand."

"Try me."

Cam blew out a long breath and decided at last to risk it. What did he have to lose? "I was—how to put it—a double agent, see, and . . . well . . . Jason found out." He searched Pee Wee's face for a sign of disapproval, but found only encouragement that he continue. "Anyway, Jason took my backpack, only he thought it was Buddy's. Thought it had Buddy's spoils, see, and he tied it up in a tree. As a prank. You know." Why was he defending Jason? Or hiding the truth about Buddy?

"You mean your flute is out there where the fire is?"

Cam swallowed hard and nodded. "Mick was trying to get it when . . . when . . ." He looked up at the counselor, his eyes welling suddenly. "I had to stop him, don't you see? I tried. I did. But I only made it worse."

"Mick?" Pee Wee said gently. His hands were warm on Cam's bare shoulders. "Why, Cam? Why did you have to stop him?"

"Not Mick. Jason!" The name flew out of his mouth before he could retrieve it. There. He'd told. He *was* a traitor after all.

"What was he doing? Please, Cam. Tell me."

Cam shook his head. "It doesn't matter. Not really. It wasn't *his* fault. It was that stupid war."

"Game," Pee Wee corrected.

"No. War." Cam drew himself up tall and held Pee Wee's gaze. "It was never a game. Not to Buddy and Jason. And not to the rest of us who got dragged into it."

"But what were you fighting for?"

Cam thought for a long moment. "Our Selves," he said at last. "As in Self. With a capital *S*." He searched for a glimmer of understanding in Pee Wee's eyes but found none and knew he couldn't explain further. It was just one of those things, he thought. You had to be there.

It was well past taps time when the fire fighters, ragged and weary, gave the all clear. The captain told Pee Wee he'd be back in the morning to talk to Mountain Man and the boys involved. Cam, alone in Olympus except for the counselor, fell into a restless sleep. He awoke once before dawn to the sound of soft snoring above him, and, reassured, drifted off until reveille.

He was just throwing back his covers when Mountain Man stopped by the tent, his face still flushed from his effort on the bugle. "Up and at 'em," he said. "I want to see all you guys down on the playing field. Pronto."

Pee Wee rolled out of his bunk to accept a black trash bag from the camp director. "You want Cam, too?" he asked.

"Anyone involved in the fire. We've got some heavy-duty talking to do. A thing like this happens, there's gotta be consequences."

Cam fussed over his sleeping bag, smoothing out the wrinkles. He swallowed hard. Maybe they'd all get sent home. He could think of worse things—for himself anyway. And he doubted that Whaler and Mick would be too upset. But what about Buddy? His dad was bound to come down hard on him. Too hard. And Jason's folks were gone for the whole summer, making the rounds of regional art fairs. They wouldn't be jumping for joy about changing their plans—if Mountain Man was able to track them down.

Dressing hurriedly in his red Wisconsin T-shirt and flowered shorts, Cam stole glances at the others.

"You *wouldn't,*" Mick said, snickering at the combination.

"Why not? I like 'em." There, Cam thought. It's not so hard to tell them what I really think. He tried not to stare as the others undressed.

Mick, Buddy, and Whaler sported a few bandages on their arms and legs. Jason, his hands swathed in white and his neck and face checkered with red blisters and gauze squares, hadn't fared as well.

"You okay?" Cam said.

"Just great," Jason replied. "Never felt better."

"No, really."

Jason ignored him and said to Pee Wee, "Think you could help with my clothes?"

Pee Wee was inspecting the contents of the garbage sack, and did not reply. A grin lit his face.

"Pee Wee," Jason said, his tone insistent.

"I will," Cam offered. Ignoring Jason's grimace, he peeled the pajama top off over Jason's head. Then he rummaged through Jason's gym bag and withdrew a black Midnight Vandals T-shirt. "This okay?"

"Fine." Jason endured Cam's dressing him, mumbling a grudging "thanks" as Cam crouched down to tie his shoes.

Pee Wee tapped Cam's shoulder. "I think this belongs to you," he said, handing him the garbage sack.

Cam's pulse quickened as he hefted the weight at the bottom. "Is it . . . ?" He couldn't finish, afraid to even hope that it might be his flute.

Pee Wee grinned. "See for yourself."

Cam opened the bag and withdrew his gray backpack, damp but otherwise unharmed.

"Hey!" Jason said. "I thought that was Buddy's."

"Gimme a break." Buddy rolled his eyes. Mick and Whaler hung over Cam's shoulder as he pulled the flute case out and cracked it open.

"Here," Mick said. "Let me help." He cradled the velvet-lined case while Cam, with trembling fingers, fitted the joints.

"You really play that thing?" Whaler said.

"You should hear him. He's incredible." Pee Wee smiled encouragement and Cam managed a single tentative note on the instrument.

"Cammy one note," Jason said.

"Uh-uh, man. You're wrong." Buddy edged into the circle. "Pee Wee's telling the truth. He's awesome."

"You've heard him? No fair." Whaler pretended to pout. "How 'bout playing something for us?"

Cam's gaze connected with Pee Wee's. He licked his lips. His pulse raced, and his throat went dry. Still, he positioned the instrument and closed his eyes, praying for the breath, the fingering, the wings to let himself soar. Then he began the Mozart, tentatively at first but quickly gaining momentum. It was coming up soon—

the hard part. And suddenly he was—it was—there. All of it. All the measures he'd agonized over for months, flowing one after the other exactly as the Master had written them. Cam's joy swelled in his chest. This was different, better, than he'd ever imagined. What had changed? he wondered as tears stung his eyelids.

Blinking them back, he glimpsed the faces of the other guys: Buddy, slack jawed, a faraway look in his eyes; Jason, head cocked to one side, smirking his own brand of approval; Whaler, grinning with childlike delight; and Mick, lips pressed firmly together, eyes shining, as if reflecting Cam's joy back to him.

When he finally stopped playing, no one spoke for a long moment. Then everyone did at once. "The secret's out now," Pee Wee said. "Everyone in camp must have heard *that.*"

Cam grinned sheepishly. He was just shuffling through his music, looking for an encore piece, when Mountain Man rapped on the door. "Thought I told you guys to hustle," he said. "First things first."

Cam laid his flute on his bunk, amazed to see it resting there in full view of the others. He felt like a red chameleon that refused to turn green in the grass, bold and proud and visible at last. Flinging open the door, he marched out into the new day's sunlight, felt the others close behind.

"You think Mountain Man'll send us home?" Buddy asked as they crossed the service road. The brown playing field stood in sharp contrast to the swath of blackened ridge beyond the Swamp. "Come on, Pee Wee. I gotta know."

Pee Wee shook his head. "I doubt it. He said there'd be consequences. But I think he means cleaning up after the fire. Stuff like that."

Buddy breathed out his gratitude. "That's a relief." Cam was surprised to realize that he shared Buddy's reaction.

As if on cue, everyone stopped on the ridge overlooking the ball field. The captain of the fire department and Mountain Man were motioning for them to come down. Jason bit his lip, and toed the dust with his sneaker. Mick wiped the corners of his eyes, while Buddy held his chin up defiantly. Only Whaler looked impassive.

"Come on," Cam said. "What're you turkeys waiting for?" Without glancing back, he slid down the ridge.

"Hey!" Jason called. "What's your hurry?"

Cam rejected the shrug he figured Jason would expect. "The sooner I get this over with," he said, "the sooner I can go practice." Then, without glancing back to check anyone's reaction, he set off across the grass in his red T-shirt and flowered shorts.